MORTON
3/15

$c5/5/19$

LoL $c/15$

4 JUN 2016

0 2 APR 2016

2 0 MAY 2016

2 3 JUL 2016

2 2 SEP 2016   2 7 JUN 2015

BRU 10/17

0 4 JAN 2016

2 2 DEC 2015

2 9 AUG 2018

2 0 JUL 2015

2 9 OCT 2016

SPECIAL MESSAGE TO READERS

ROGUE'S RUN

Johnny Richards is no gunfighter, in the true sense, but he is considered the fastest gun alive. He learned his prowess not in the badlands of Texas but the big top of Fraley's Frontier Circus. If anyone figures that puts him at a disadvantage though, they're in for a mighty big surprise. Speed and accuracy are necessary in both callings, the only difference being that real life requires real bullets — and real victims. And they begin to pile up fast . . .

TYLER HATCH

ROGUE'S
RUN

Complete and Unabridged

LINFORD
Leicester

First published in Great Britain in 2012 by
Robert Hale Limited
London

First Linford Edition
published 2013
by arrangement with
Robert Hale Limited
London

A catalogue record for this book is available
from the British Library.

ISBN 978–1–4448–1669–3

Published by
F. A. Thorpe (Publishing)
Anstey, Leicestershire

Set by Words & Graphics Ltd.
Anstey, Leicestershire
Printed and bound in Great Britain by
T. J. International Ltd., Padstow, Cornwall

This book is printed on acid-free paper

Prologue

When he regained consciousness, the first thing he saw was four men hanging from the big cottonwood that shaded the barn.

No! Not four *men:* three men and *the boy!*

The barn was now no more than a heap of smouldering ashes with one or two charred frame uprights canted towards the rising sun.

So Hammond did it after all, the son of a bitch! Goddamnit! He'd — done — it!'

Wounded as he was, he had managed to prop himself up on one elbow, congealing blood from his headwound blinding him in one eye. His breath was ragged. Pain coursed through his chest. He tried to see what other havoc Hammond and his crew had left behind but fell back weakly,

1

fingers clawing into the gravel as he tumbled away from the world . . .

Into welcome oblivion.

1

Hellboy

Three years later . . .

Martin Sands bunched his shoulder muscles and drove the axe blade into the iron-hard root of the massive tree stump he had been trying to remove for five days now.

The blade skidded off, lashed back and hacked through the loose cuff of his mud-stained trousers. The sun-hot metal of the flat side of the blade seared across his bare skin and he jumped out of the hole, tossing the axe away from him in a fit of temper. *Five goddamn days!*

And now the goddamn axe had nearly taken his goddamn leg off! If the lousy blade had held an edge better he'd be bleeding to death right now — *No!* If the lousy blade had held its edge, he would have cut halfway through that stubborn root! Well, that was *it! Call it quits!*

He was working himself into the ground! Literally! If — when — he finally got that stump out, they could just topple him into the hole and start shovelling back the soil . . . because he would be worn out and uncaring . . .

This hardrock spread had beaten him. What happened to that stubborn streak you were so proud of? Never give in — keep coming back — win, no matter how long it took . . .

Yeah! He knew the answer but felt guilty even just thinking it: *Joanna* — all he wanted to do was please her and so he made concessions. *Maybe too many* . . . . But he was going to stick with this one, hell or high water.

Sweat pouring down his begrimed, naked chest, he wiped a hand across his face, lifted his hat, tousled his sweat-soaked fair hair. Above his left temple the hair clumped and slid away an inch or so, revealing the groove of an old scar, deep enough so he could almost lay his little finger in the furrow across the flesh.

It still gave him the occasional headache — but not as many headaches as trying to clear this lousy hunk of dirt! Hell, he'd never make it by prove-up! He'd either be dead, or a wrung-out useless stringbean — and still not have the spread he had hoped to build up. *For himself and Joanna.*

'To hell with it!' he murmured aloud, reaching for the canteen of water that hung by its strap from a bush. He took a mouthful, spat it out. Hot! He could make coffee just by pouring in a handful of beans! He tossed the canteen away, started to kick the stack of tools but held his cocked boot at the last moment.

Stupid! That won't do any good!

No — only thing that'll do some good now is to find some way of getting that four-acre block on the rise above Benbow Creek. Joanna really liked it, but she knew there was not enough money, so he had decided to try a quarter-section under prove-up rules, get it liveable by the time the wedding day came around, sell it at a later date and hope the Benbow Creek land would be still available. *Not damn likely, though!*

But *if that rumour Benjamin Bodie had passed on only yesterday was true — there just could be an outside chance!*

Hell, it was the *only* chance — short of robbing a bank — to get the money. He felt himself tense: it could be risky, though. Not just the deed itself but if he pulled it off there was bound to be publicity and 'someone' could make the connection to those earlier years when he was better known on the Rodeo Circuit.

It was chancey, all right, but the only way . . .

And just to make it real easy, he knew damn well Joanna wouldn't approve.

★ ★ ★

'*No!*'

It was as emphatic and as resounding as he had expected. He had even pictured how she would look when she said it: that lovely, slightly triangular face with the silk-smooth skin, the cheeks faintly tinged with pink, the trade-mark inch or so of unruly blonde curls brushing her smooth forehead, the perfectly-arched eyebrows drawing together, a few creases then, and the sky-blue eyes narrowing. Now the full lips thinned out, pursed slightly as they came together in visual disapproval, her head shaking side to side, slow and insistent.

'Jo, I can tame that stallion! I know I can — I've spent some time down at the town corrals and studied him. I know how he moves, can see the rippling of his shoulder and chest muscles when one of the other broncs comes too close — the way his lips peel back!' He stepped forward, took her by the elbows, but while she looked up into his face — he was just over six feet tall and she was maybe five-six at most

— her expression didn't change. Nor did her tensed body. 'I can do it, Jo! I can read his signs now, anticipate his moves — you've got to believe me. And with the Benbow land as the prize — or $3,000 cash — we can get a right good start to our married life, whichever one we choose.'

He sounded enthusiastic without any conscious effort, but he knew he was fighting a losing battle. Then she said the words he had been dreading, though he knew it was inevitable she would say them:

'Have you forgotten what happened to Jason?'

She said it bitterly, through her white teeth, and right then he didn't care at all for the way she looked. But he tightened his grip on her arms, not noticing how she winced at the increased pressure.

'I haven't forgotten Jace! I never will . . . I'd never have met you if I hadn't known him.'

'Then how can you even *think* of

entering this stupid competition!' She almost stamped her foot but restrained herself in time, eyes beginning to fill at the memory of her brother when they had brought him back from the corrals, bloody and broken after the horse they called 'Demon' had stomped and savaged him.

Sands swallowed. 'Jo — that damn horse should never have been in that corral. Everyone knows now it either jumped from the 'untamed' corral into the one where the half-broke mounts were waiting . . . or someone let it in, some half-drunk trail hand's idea of a joke, mebbe. It hurts to say it, but Jace was a fool to even attempt to throw a saddle on Demon.'

'How dare you call my brother a fool!'

Man, he thought she was going to take a swing at him, but emotion took over first and tears coursed down her face, the sobbing started and she didn't resist when he folded her in his arms, her body now willowy and weak as he

9

held her, feeling the warmth of her tears already through his shirt.

'Jo! — Jo! I — knew it would stir memories of Jason but, well, you know what he was like. He'd see it's the only chance for us to get that creek-bottom land and he'd say, 'Go for your life, *amigo*. Go get it done!''

The sobbing continued, eased more quickly than he expected. She took a half-step back and dabbed at her eyes, blew her nose and then looked steadily at him. *He had upset her but she was trying to be fair.*

'Martin — I — I know you're right about how Jason would see it — but Jace is dead and now it's how I see it! If you succeeded, yes, it would get us that land — or get *me* that land! I mean, I wouldn't want it if you . . . weren't there to . . . share it with me, or if, if you were there but — couldn't help build our dream of a small ranch where we could raise our family because that damn horse had . . . crippled you!'

He pulled her close again, feeling like

a son of a bitch, chewing on one end of his flourishing frontier moustache. 'Hon — I wouldn't even think about it if I knew of any other way. It's not as if I'm some green-horn. Bronc-busting was my living for years — I broke my first horse before I was fourteen and — '

'But it's a long time since you worked at it professionally! Oh, yes, you've broken in plenty of horses for ranch work and so on but you haven't made a living as a rodeo hand, or breaking in wild-eyed mustangs to entertain a blood-hungry audience for — how many years now?'

'Three,' he said tersely. *An exact count!* And the way she looked at him he knew she'd already known how long when she asked the question.

'Then you must see how dangerous it could be for you to tackle this . . . thing they call 'Hellboy'!'

'It's not something you forget, Jo! It's bred into you. My father had it, and two of my uncles. It runs in the family . . . '

11

'Not *our* family!' she snapped huskily, and immediately gripped his arms hard. 'Oh, Martin! I know I'm being bitchy now but it's because I'm so afraid for you! That horse is a terrible animal: he's maimed two men at least, bitten fingers off one of his handlers, kicked corrals and livery stalls to matchwood . . . '

'That's why they call him 'Hellboy'. Jo, there's no way I can make prove-up on that quarter-section — and even if I did, it's lousy hardrock. You have to admit that.'

She hesitated, then nodded briefly. 'I — know.'

He took a deep breath, leaned down and kissed her lightly on the cheek. 'Well . . . ? This is a way out of the fix, so what d'you say? It's our future, Jo . . . '

'You don't need to remind me of that!' She shredded the damp handkerchief, looked up again, her blue eyes swimming now, but she nodded just once and he folded her in against him.

'I suppose it *is* the only way, but I can't help — '

'Start thinking of what we're gonna call our first child — pick a boy's name and a girl's, just to be sure.'

She stepped back and pounded his chest in mock anger. 'We're not even married yet!'

'Pays to be prepared . . . I'm ready to say 'I do' any time.'

'Not just any time, you impatient man! June 6th at the Episcopalian Church in Flagstaff — and not before.'

'Hell, it'll be worth the wait,' he said aloud and she drew back her head and frowned slightly.

'I should hope so!'

'Sure it will — that Benbow Creek parcel will be fine land to raise our family on, Jo. We'll have about seven kids, I reckon, and — '

'*Who'll* have seven children?'

'Well, I ain't built that way, but it takes two, you know.'

'Oh! You exasperating man! But I do love you, Martin Sands! Even though I know you'll turn me prematurely grey with all your wild schemes.'

'Don't worry. Grey hair'll suit you just fine.'

★　★　★

'Hey, Walt! Come take a look at this.'

Walt Derby finished strapping on his spurs and sauntered across the bunkhouse to the table where Tad Macrossan had spread out a newspaper. Derby was big, had the hard look of a man who had spent his entire life riding the range. He leaned down to look over Tad's shoulder, a man tall as himself but stringbean lean.

'What . . . ? Aw, hell, I thought you had a picture of one of them new dancehall gals from that troupe that just hit town. What do they call themselves?'

'The Hi-Kickers,' Derby said without looking up, and slapped a hand down on to the paper spread out. 'No, this is that *Big Sky Clarion* they publish in Cheyenne, once a month — they call it the 'Frontier Round-up'. Someone said Bat Masterson writes it, but I don't b'lieve that. Anyway, that big rodeo prize everyone's been talkin' about went off at Lone Pine in Arizona. Someone finally rid that good of ol' Hellboy into the ground. I recall that killer bronc when Mitch Barnaby first roped him and brought him down from the Muggyown. Must be all of three years ago now.' He shook his head slowly. 'Nearly kicked the barn to pieces, you recollect? Figured someone woulda shot him before this.'

'Yeah, well, anyone rode that damn jughead to a standstill must've earned his prize, that's for sure.'

Walt lifted one hand. 'Got a picture of him here — didn't get off easy. Busted arm, couple broken ribs, head injuries. It says they had to cut his hair short to stitch up his scalp, even shaved off his moustache so they could work on his nose and teeth.'

'Jesus! He must've wanted that prize money bad!'

15

Derby turned the page around so Walt could see the grainy picture properly. 'Martin Sands. Story says he wants this piece of land they're offerin' so's he can get married.' He put on a drawling hillbilly voice: 'Aw, now ain't that cute?' Then he almost spat. 'Goddamn trash they print these days, when — ' His voice trailed away and suddenly he grabbed the page, crumpling it as he took it over to the window, then smoothed it out so he could see the picture better. 'Hey! You take a good look at this?'

Macrossan nodded slowly. 'Wondered if you'd recognize him . . . '

Derby's knuckles were white where they held the newspaper. 'Martin Sands . . . ? Dunno that name but — by God! short hair and without the moustache . . . ' He snapped his head up, looked at Macrossan. 'It's him, ain't it! John goddamn Richards! After all this time!'

'I figure so, too.'

There were two grainy, grey pictures

of Martin Sands, one as he was *before* he rode Hellboy, complete with long hair brushed around his ears, side whiskers and droopy frontier moustache framing a smile, and the other after the Flagstaff Hospital doctors had shaved him, given him a close haircut and patched him up some: he looked forlorn, suffering. The caption read: *Was it worth it?*

And the journalist's text answered: 'Martin Sands gives a resounding *'Yea!'* Hurt, but happy, Martin is a very private man, now betrothed to the beautiful Joanna Craig, who regular readers will recall was *Queen of Spring* in the Flagstaff Annual Festival two years running. But read on and learn more about this frontier romance between the rugged bronc-buster and the beauty queen — all with a fairy-tale ending, my friends! Your reporter has learned exclusively that the marital knot will be tied this June 6th at the . . . '

Walt Derby who was reading ahead of Tad Macrossan, snatched the paper away and threw it on the floor in disgust. 'Damn daisy like him oughta know! Says they gonna be married June 6th in Flagstaff which is only a couple weeks off.'

'Yeah, paper's a few weeks old, last month's, I think — Richards oughta be lookin' decent again by the weddin' day . . . '

Derby's big mouth drew into a thin line. 'I wouldn't bet on it!' His eyes were hard points of steel. Tad snapped his head up.

'What you got in mind . . . ?'

'Not me — it'll be what Greg has in mind . . . We'll have to tell him.'

'Sure, but we'd never get to Flagstaff in time!'

'They run stages from Laramie.' Derby hitched his gunbelt, leaving his thumbs hooked in the leather. 'You think Greg won't want to follow through on this? First chance to nail that son of a bitch in five years?'

'Yeah, guess so. Christ, he'll do a backflip — wonder what he'll say?'

18

"Bring me the bastard's ears!" That's what he'll say.' Derby growled. 'Like to bet them's his exact words?'

Macrossan shook his head, studying the picture in the now crumpled paper. It was more difficult to make out and he ran a tongue over his lips as he looked up and said quietly, 'We better be damn sure we ain't makin' any mistake, Walt.'

"'Cause he calls himself 'Martin Sands'? Hell, the marshals woulda stuck him with that name after he gave evidence at Linus's trial.' Walt Derby slapped the back of his hand against the newspaper. 'Nah — that's Johnny Richards, all right, and if he thinks he suffered after ridin' Hellboy, he dunno crap from coffee.'

2

Do or Die

Greg Hammond was a man in his forties, looked well fed, but there was a tinge of greyness about his mouth and a kind of fleeting dullness in his eyes. He was thinning up top but wasn't vain about it, hadn't tried to hide it in any way, though he had used the regular diversion of a grey-speckled moustache fringing his upper lip.

His face was round, streaked with a random network of long-healed scars — which may have been caused by a past gun-whipping — nose showing a fine tracery of blue-and-red veins. But Greg Hammond didn't drink to excess: he was a man who always had to feel he was in complete control of his mind, or any situation.

Now he raised his strange green eyes

from the crumpled newspaper and looked steadily at Walt Derby and Tad Macrossan as they stood silently across the big desk from him in the ranch office. 'Too far and too close.'

His voice had an edge of breathlessness and Walt and Tad exchanged puzzled glances, then looked back quickly to Hammond as he went on, speaking in that gasping way.

'*Too far* to get to Flagstaff in time because the wedding is *too damn close!* You get it now?'

Derby nodded, Tad a shade behind. 'Sure, Greg. But I reckon we could mebbe just about make it in time.'

He let whatever else he was about to say drift off as the rancher shook his head slowly.

'*Mebbes* an' *just abouts* ain't good enough. We'll do it another way — find Chandler and Jones.'

After a short silence, Derby asked, '*Chiricahua* Jones . . . ?'

'Who the hell else you think I meant? He's Chandler's pard, ain't he?'

'Yeah, sure, Greg. I just — well, I mean they're gunfighters an' damn good, but you haven't used 'em for a while, an' me and Tad ain't no slouches.'

'No, you're pretty good, or you wouldn't still be working for me, but Hank Chandler and Chiricahua Jones are in Prescott — hop, step and a jump from Flagstaff.'

As usual, Hammond said no more: *let 'em work it out for themselves, keep their brains from turning to slush.*

Tad Macrossan shifted his weight from one foot to the other. 'If you're still offerin' that re-ward, boss — '

'It's a *standing* offer, Tad,' Hammond explained tiredly. *Dumb bastards he employed!* 'Means it's waiting there, on offer, till someone claims it.'

'Yeah, well — that's what I mean. Me and Walt, we been your trouble-shooters for a long time now and — ' He glanced at Derby for some kind of back-up but Walt remained silent: *let Tad step in the dung now he's already opened his mouth . . .*

Macrossan frowned and cleared his throat. 'Well, we could do with that reward money, you know?'

'I know what you mean, damnit. But Chandler and Jones are on the spot. The money's theirs. You boys'll still be pulling down your pay.'

Yeah! As ranch-hands! thought Tad, and maybe Derby thought the same, but neither spoke out loud.

Hammond was writing fast on a notepad he had taken from a drawer. 'Go into town and send this wire to Bailey in Prescott. He'll find Chandler and Jones and I'll send 'em orders. We've got an old code Linus used; they'll savvy what's to be done, all right.'

Tad Macrossan licked his lips. 'Er — we oughta make sure there's no mistake, boss . . . I mean, I hope it is Richards in that picture, but it's been five years.'

Greg Hammond gave him a bleak look.

'It could be *fifty* years and I'd still

know that son of a bitch!' He waved the paper, thrust it across the table. 'Get that wire off — pronto.'

★ ★ ★

It seemed that most of the county had turned out for the wedding.

After all, Flagstaff didn't often see a genuine 'hero' and an ex-Queen-of-the-Carnival tying the marital knot.

And the truth was so many folk were so relieved to know that Hellboy had finally been defeated — at least for now! — that the rodeo company decided to foot the bill for one big celebration. *Come one, come all . . .*

The main focus, of course, was on the church itself, an average building of clapboard with a small steeple and a brass bell that was said to have rung the alarm at Fort Carbine when General Taylor Boothe finally defeated Chief One Hand almost thirty years earlier.

The church was packed tight with townsfolk and gawkers from all over the county, standing on tables at the windows and, in some cases, on men's shoulders, bringing giggles and embarrassed squeals from many a maiden in her Sunday best — although it happened to be a Saturday.

Jo was breathtakingly beautiful in her bridal gown, fussed over by her aunts and cousins, two of whom were her maids-of-the-day. Martin Sands was uncomfortable in his pearl grey suit, felt somehow naked without his moustache. His mouth was still stiff and sore from the work they had done on his teeth; there would be a fine tracery of scars later. He'd had to pad the inside of his hat, too, they had cut his hair so short, but the scalp wounds had healed pretty well.

His best man was Harvey Moll, who had once been Sands' partner in a mustang-gathering business. Harve had turned to the horse-trading side with considerable success.

'You've got yourself a real beauty, Marty. How you did it beats me.'

'Beats me, too, but I don't aim to let go of her!'

Then the preacher called for order and the organ began the well known strains of the *Bridal March* and Sands sucked down a deep breath, felt in the lower left-hand front pocket of the silk vest to make sure the ring was there, and turned to face the aisle where all eyes were now focused. He felt he and Harvey simply didn't exist for the few minutes it took Joanna and her maids to make the journey down the aisle to the altar where the serious-looking (and nervous, Sands thought) young preacher waited, a stiff smile on his face, fumbling with his leather-bound book.

The ceremony went smoothly with only a couple of hiccups when the preacher lost his place in the text. Then came the moment when he said, 'I now pronounce you man and wife. Martin, you may now kiss your bride!'

A murmur and a few smothered giggles ran through the attentive congregation as Martin Sands swallowed, stepped forward and with shaky hands lifted Joanna's veil. She was absolutely *glowing*, he thought, as her warm smile welcomed him. He could hear her excited breath as she lifted her face towards his.

He slipped his hands about her waist and —

A gun crashed like a clap of thunder through the church and Joanna was torn from his grasp with a choked-off scream as she reeled into the startled preacher, who grabbed at her instinctively, and the pair of them collapsed at Sands' feet.

He was frozen, shocked into immobility, seeing only the brilliant splash of blood against the bodice of the silk and lace bridal gown . . .

'I now pronounce you *widower*, you son of a bitch!'

Despite the echoes of the gunfire and the roar, screams and shouts, Martin Sands heard the words clearly, and, still stunned, he spun towards the front door of the church where powdersmoke made hazy some of the faces there.

Just as he glimpsed a vaguely familiar face, Harvey Moll grabbed his arm and dragged him to his knees.

'Get down, you idiot! You're his next target!'

'No! He's *mine!*' Sands corrected Moll and wrenched free, charging into the milling, surging crowds, making for the turmoil at the front door where the gunman was battering his way out into the churchyard.

'Stop him!' Sands yelled hoarsely, eyes wild, hands thrusting roughly and uncaringly.

But no one tried to stop the killer — they had their own lives to think of and couldn't be blamed as they pawed and thrust at each other to get out of the way.

Teeth gritted, Sands hammered his way through, saw the killer had stopped a few yards out from the steps. People were running in all directions, but his gun was waiting for Sands to appear.

Martin dived off the steps even as the

gun blasted and a man in the fleeing congregation yelled as the bullet found him. Sands' lunge had taken him almost to the gunman, who was startled by the manoeuvre and fumbled his smoking Colt as his target swarmed towards him. Sands ducked under the gun arm, lifted swiftly, knocking the weapon skywards as it discharged. He clawed with one hand at the other's arm, drove his free fist into the sweaty face.

The head wrenched back and the hat with the concha-studded band fell off, revealing an Indian-like swarthy face, lank black hair falling across the scarred forehead.

'*Cherry Jones!*' Sands gritted in surprise.

Chiricahua — 'Cherry' — Jones, the half-breed, bared his yellow teeth and lifted a knee towards Sands' crotch. Martin only just managed to turn his thigh in time, then there was a flash in his mind of Joanna falling in her blood-splashed gown, and the murder-ous rage he hadn't known for so long roared through him.

His hand clawed into the rough-skinned throat of the 'breed, lifted him with such force that Cherry Jones's feet cleared the ground. His head was twisting from side to side, eyes bulging. His gun started to fall but Sands snatched it, flung the man from him violently.

Jones sprawled and rolled, gagging, fighting for breath, but instinctively reached for the knife in its flat sheath at the back of his neck under his loose-fitting shirt. Sands rolled, came up on to one knee and triggered. Jones skidded along the dust, but had his knife free. He swung his arm backwards, the blade glinting as it flashed in the sunlight. Without thinking, Sands fired and his bullet shattered the blade, sent the hilt spinning into a nearby flower pot.

He found his mind racing, mentally counting the shots fired — starting with the one that had cut down his bride of less than a minute . . . He figured there was one left in the Colt and he aimed swiftly and shot the writhing Jones in the middle of the face.

Then a second gun banged in two quick shots from behind a tethered buckboard in the churchyard and Martin Sands staggered, one leg buckling. He went down to his knees, spotted the gunsmoke and threw himself full length in the gravel of the church path as the second gun fired again and sent chips of bluestone spinning into his face and neck.

'Here!'

It was Harvey's voice and he tossed his own six-gun so that it landed right beside Sands. Martin, ignoring the pain in his thigh and feeling the blood squishing dropped the empty Colt, snatched up Harvey Moll's gun and fired under the buckboard at the half-hidden killer's legs.

The man collapsed as a bullet tore across both thighs, but he knew his job and despite the pain, rolled on to his belly, emptying his gun in a short, deadly volley. While Sands was rolling in turn as the lead kicked up more gravel, Hank Chandler grabbed the spokes of the buggy wheel and heaved himself up, staggering towards a slim tree a few feet away. Limping, bleeding, he clawed more or less upright, slapped the reins of the buggy team free and yelled and waved his arms. The vehicle lurched forward with a creak of leather and crack of straining timber. Chandler hopped towards the startled team and they swung in Sands' direction, charging wild-eyed now as the fear struck deep and they bolted up the gravel path.

Folk scattered everywhere and Sands was knocked off his feet as he tried to rise. Feeling the shock of his wound hammering through him now, he managed to stagger towards Chandler's tree. He had recognized the gunman and knew now he was once again a hunted man — *if* he managed to survive *this* . . .

Chandler had awkwardly tied his

neckerchief around one of his wounds and reloaded swiftly. He stepped out from behind the tree, baring his teeth and holding the gun in both hands as he saw Sands coming towards him unsteadily.

Maybe he thought Sands was still using Jones's gun, not realizing it was empty, because Hank Chandler stood free of his shelter, planted his boots as firmly as he could on his wounded legs, and lifted his reloaded Colt deliberately.

'It was a short married life, eh, Johnny-boy?'

Chandler almost laughed — then stumbled back as Sands put two shots into his body. The surprise on his face was genuine as he folded up, his own gun shooting into the ground. He twisted as he fell, landing mostly on his back, blood already dribbling from a corner of his mouth, chest heaving.

Sands shuffled forwards, looked down at him and coldly shot him through the head.

Some men crouching nearby stared,

33

saggy-mouthed, and one said,

'Goddlemighty! He's as big a killer as them two gun-slingers!'

More townsfolk came running up, all staring at this hard-faced, cold-eyed figure they had so recently known as the amiable Martin Sands, rodeo hero — and newly-wed.

But this man holding the smoking gun who they now regarded with such shock and horror was a total stranger to them.

Someone they'd never seen before.

Someone they didn't even want to know.

3

Starting Point

Sheriff Vince Starrett, a deacon of the church, had left all weapons behind when he had attended the wedding. There was no reason not to — in fact, in Starrett's way of thinking, there never was a reason to take a lethal weapon into God's house.

He was in his forties, a strict family man, and, he liked to think, a fair-minded lawman. Though some of the townsfolk figured he was no more than a fuddy-duddy, did nothing that wasn't in the law book, made few, if any, concessions, and meticulously entered every fine applied in a special book marked *County Accounts*.

He looked smart enough in his neat frock coat and iron-creased striped trousers, and with his narrow-brimmed hat perched atop his head he caught up with Martin Sands who was heading for Doc McAllister's infirmary.

'Hold up there, Martin! I say — slow down if you will!'

Sands turned slowly, his dirt-smeared face tight-lipped, his wounded leg bent a little as he took most of his weight on the other.

'Vince, whatever it is, keep it till later. All I'm interested in right now is to see if Jo's still alive — and if she's gonna stay that way.'

'Understandable, Martin, but perhaps I can ask a few questions and walk with you to the infirmary?'

'I don't aim to walk, Vince.'

Sands' words were clipped and he turned and stomped away at a surprising pace, considering he had been shot in the thigh. Starrett shook his head once and then hurried to catch up, almost jogging alongside.

'Those men you killed were known gunmen. There will be no comeback about that, though I might have reservations about the way you . . . despatched them.'

'Have all the reservations you want. They tried to kill Jo *and* me. I wasn't aiming to play pat-a-cake.'

'How — how d'you walk so fast with that bullet in you?' panted the lawman.

'I cut it out before I bandaged it.' Sands swung into McAllister's street and the sheriff hurried to catch up.

'One puzzling, and, to my mind, quite serious thing, Martin — ' Starrett slowed but if he expected Sands to do the same he was disappointed. He clamped his lips together and hurried to catch up. 'Cherry Jones called you 'Johnny'.'

That slowed Sands and he stopped, the unprepared lawman going past and having to swing back quickly.

'That could explain it then,' Sands said soberly.

'Explain what?'

'He mistook me for someone else. My name's Martin Sands, you know that — no part of it sounds like

'Johnny' to me.'

Starrett frowned and while he thought about Sands' reply, Martin went through the gate along a flower-edged path to the doctor's front door. It opened almost at once to his thundering knock and Mrs McAllister stood there, a strand of grey hair hanging over her forehead, red-smeared hands holding a kidney dish with bloody water in it.

'How is she, ma'am?' Sands snapped without preamble, already sidling past the woman into the short hallway. He knew the left branch led to the infirmary section and turned towards it.

'Just a moment, Martin! Doctor is very busy right now.'

'How — is — she? That's all I'm interested in — and if Doc's 'busy' it better had be on something to do with Jo.'

'Oh, calm down, for heaven's sake! Of course he's working on Joanna. She's a very fortunate woman. The bullet passed between two lower ribs, went straight through without touching the bone or damaging any of the important organs. She'll be laid up for a couple of weeks and will need to take it very easy for some time afterward. She paused, looking severely at Sands. 'Very easy, you understand, Martin! Honeymoon or not.'

He nodded jerkily. 'I'll look after her. Can I see her?'

'Well, it's hardly feasible. She's under chloroform right now . . .'

'I just want to see her, damnit!' He swung away down the pasaage to the infirmary and Mrs McAllister made an exasperated sound and followed quickly.

Vince Starrett, shaking his head, followed, briskly and importantly, feeling annoyed that he had lost control of what had started out to be a brisk and, he had hoped, informative interrogation.

For all his affiliation with the church and his fuddy-duddy ways, Vince Starrett was a stickler for law and order and was not afraid to enforce it where he considered it necessary . . . backed-up by his six-gun and a leather-covered truncheon he carried.

He was forced to wait while Sands stayed with the Doctor — against McAllister's wishes, but there was no shifting Martin Sands and it was over an hour later before he had Sands in his law office on Kilburn Street with the street door closed.

He hadn't gotten anywhere with his questions so far: all Sands would say was that it was obvious the gunmen had mistaken him for someone else.

'But you *knew* them, Martin! You called them by name!'

'I've seen 'em around.'

'They're notorious outlaws and have been so for a lot of years — but never up in this neck of the woods. How is it you 'saw them around'? And where?'

Sands drummed his fingers on the desk edge, had loosened his tie, but still felt uncomfortable in his wedding suit. 'You got tobacco and papers?'

'I don't smoke,' the sheriff said but brought out a round leather container with a tight-fitting lid which he removed and proffered the container to Sands. 'I've had these cheroots for some time — confiscated them from a man carrying stolen goods — but the container is air-tight. They should be all right.'

'They'll do.' Sands took one and Starrett passed him a small tin of vestas. When the cheroot was alight and Sands had taken a couple of draws, the sheriff said:

'I believe those two men were settling an old score, with you, Martin. I'd like you to tell me about it.' He held up a hand quickly as Sands made to speak. 'It happened in my town: attempted murder, two killings. You were involved, and I — want — an — explanation — I mean now, Martin.'

Sands puffed smoke, looking steadily at this somewhat effeminate man who had a strong touch of iron in him that surprised most everybody who had cause to ruffle his feathers.

Hell, everything had blown up now, anyway; if they'd sent two killers like

41

Chandler and Jones, then the whole damned thing was about to start all over again! He had Jo to consider, too. There was no time to get in touch with Bowen but he was going to need help, a lot of help, and right now it looked like Starrett was the only one who might be able to give it to him . . .

He blew a long plume of smoke, watched it rise towards the ceiling, then lowered his gaze to Starrett's face. The lawman's face was grim, unbending, but patient . . . or was it just plain stubborn . . . ?

'It can't go beyond this office, Vince. Not one word of what I'm about to tell you.'

Starrett pursed his lips. 'Well, I believe I will reserve the right to decide that, Martin. No, no, it's only fair. This is my town and you've brought death and violence to it. You owe me an explanation.'

Sands wanted to hit him but merely said curtly, 'When you agree to keep it confidential.'

'I already told you I will decide about that once I hear what you have to say.'

Sands stood abruptly. 'G'day, Vince. You can find me at Doc McAllister's if you want me.'

He had his hand on the door when Starrett spoke, a snappy, steel edge to his usually calm voice now. 'Very well, Martin — if you feel so strongly. But I must advise that if there is any breach of the law I will — '

He stopped because Sands laughed — hard and brief.

'Breach of the law!' He limped back to his chair and sat down again, thumbing back his hat. 'You just made a joke, whether you know it or not.' He took a long drag on the cheroot and exhaled. 'All right. We'll have to go back quite a few years — when I was known as John Richards . . . sometimes, called 'Johnny'.'

'Yes, let's do that,' Vince Starrett said firmly, and the man everyone in Flagstaff knew as 'Martin Sands' began to speak:

* * *

John Richards grew up with horses, guns and hard-living men.

But not on any ranch or frontier farm: he lived and travelled in a circus that roamed all over the pioneer lands, entertaining people from all walks of life, but mostly concentrating on small but well established towns within a day or so's ride of ranches and outflung settlers. He lived with his father, also named John, and his father's brothers, Uncle Ben and Uncle Wes. His mother had died when he was three years old and he barely recalled her. Some of the circus womenfolk were motherly to him at times, but mostly he lived in the company of men — and from an early age they treated him as being much older than he was. He was expected to pull his weight: if he ate grub paid for with money they earned at the circus, then it was only fair he contributed: washing the dishes, grooming the mounts, chopping firewood . . .

He gladly did these chores given him, making him feel growed-up: mucking-out the stables, curry-combing the horses, feeding them and stacking the sacks of grain — although such work tired him out at first, it also helped build muscles.

He graduated to helping his father set up traps for mustangs, built corrals and fought the wild animals as they were roped and brought to the nubbing post — then had the breaking-in saddle thrown across their backs and were turned loose with or without a rider hanging on grimly. More than once Johnny didn't let go of the head rope quickly enough and he sailed clear over the top rails . . . That also was a lesson learned — and well remembered.

But the performing horses and the tricks they were taught were only one part of the circus troupe's show, which lasted about two hours, slightly less for matinees.

Uncle Ben was one of the trick riders, together with a red-haired girl named Flame who performed in a glittering, skimpy costume, so it was one of the most popular acts. Uncle Wes had his own act, using guns: pistols, rifles and sometimes a shotgun. Flame would ride around the ring on a specially trained palomino called Candy and Wes Richards shot targets out of her hands and hair and, sometimes, (if she was in a good mood and feeling a mite reckless) from between her white teeth as a grand finale.

Many times, Uncle Wes's act was performed out of doors, weather permitting. He used .22 calibre weapons with reduced loads in the cartridges so that any stray bullets (mighty rare!) would drop quickly before endangering any of the audience.

It was only natural that a fast-growing lad like Johnny should show as much interest in guns as he did horses and other animals. His father and Uncle Ben had passed on their knowledge of trapping and training wild horses, and now it was Wes's turn to impart knowledge about firearms.

Johnny had only erratic schooling and when Wes handed him some well-worn technical books and told him to study up on the development and workings of firing mechanisms, from the clumsy matchlock through flash-pan, flintlock, separate percussion cap, to the self-contained cartridge, he groaned, figuring it would be just like being in school. But he found true interest in the old but precise drawings and the information, each section demonstrated for him by Wes with his excellent collection of guns.

Working in .22 calibre meant working with rimfire cartridges. The knowledgable Wes also taught him about centre-fire cartridges in the larger calibres.

'You'll want to do some huntin' some day that's gonna bag you somethin' bigger'n a chipmunk or possum, boy — and, even a time when you'll need a .38 or .45 for defence.'

In his teens at the time, that got Johnny's interest pronto . . .

He turned out to be a natural shot with revolver or rifle (accuracy wasn't too necessary with a shotgun!) and could group his shots more tightly than Wes himself, time and time again.

'That boy's gonna be able to knock a shoo-fly off an apple-pan Dowdy without even disturbin' the sugar on the crust, mark my words,' Wes told Johnny's father proudly.

'You just make sure he never has to pick a target that's gonna shoot back,' John Richards Senior said, a little worry showing in his eyes: perhaps he saw something in young Johnny that Wes and Ben didn't — but he didn't want to consciously put a name to it right then . . .

To keep his act interesting, because the show, on its endless circuit, returned to previously visited towns and played to the same audience over and over, Wes developed his Fast Draw Shoot-out act.

Part of his act had been for Flame to throw six glass medicine phials into the air while he drew his gun, shoot them before they fell to the ground and have the smoking revolver back in his holster as the last shards of glass pattered down. The phials were each filled with coloured water so they made spectacular little explosions in mid-air.

It was one of the most popular acts on the programme and then Wes took it a step further: he had trained young Johnny in the fast draw and the kid picked it up as swiftly and expertly as he had everything else he had been taught.

They staged a mock gunfight, one or other playing the bad man to get it going — using blanks, naturally. It wasn't definitely decided who would win each time: it was random luck at the time of the act.

To Wes's surprise, and maybe a little chagrin, Johnny beat him seven or eight times out of ten. He would always act surprised and turn to the audience, while gesturing to Johnny as the winner:

'Folks, this little rogue here has come back to haunt me! I taught him all he knows — and darn me if he don't know how to beat me at my own game . . . Come on, now! An extra big hand for young Rogue Richards! Fastest gun on the circuit! Maybe fastest gun — anywhere . . . '

Johnny was flushed and excited at the reception and the way folk stopped him on the street to shake his hand and pat his back. Then John Senior's fears were realized . . .

It was only a matter of time before someone with a real mean streak and who fancied his own fast draw, threw down the kind of challenge that Johnny couldn't walk away from.

He was a raw-boned, trail-stained man, in a big wide-brimmed hat that had a frayed edge, his crooked mouth partially hidden by a drooping black moustache. He looked like a Mexican *vaquero* and it turned out he went by the name of Rayo, a corruption of a Spanish word for 'lightning'.

But despite his looks and liking for Spanish names, he spoke with a strong Southern accent.

As he often did when they arrived in a new town, Johnny wore a fancy beaded and fringed cowboy outfit down the street, just to attract attention and remind folks the circus was in town and aiming to give as many shows as possible before moving on. He never felt comfortable in the embroidered shirt and tight pants, nor even the decorated half-boots with the embossing highlighted in bright colours.

So when someone called out, '*Hey, Fancypants*', he knew damn well who they meant.

He paused, working up a smile, figuring it was some local going to exchange a few wisecracks with him.

Instead, he found Rayo in his sweat-grimy range clothes standing there with run-over boots planted firmly in the dirt of Main Street, Grady Crossing, Texas. His hands were on his hips above the butts of his twin guns that looked worn but well-oiled.

'Howdy,' Johnny said, grinning but feeling the cold knot in his belly, sensing that this wasn't going to be some light challenge so Rayo could show off. 'You comin' to tonight's show?'

'I ain't interested in 'tonight's show'!' Rayo said with a grouchy snarl. 'I'm interested in a show right here an' now! You an' me! You're s'posed to be half-brother to a bolt of lightnin' . . . well, my name's Lightnin' an' I ain't got a brother' an' I sure as hell wouldn't want you as one!'

There was a growing audience now, some of the women and even a few men showing signs of worry.

'Aw, it's just an act to advertise their show,' someone remarked, his words bringing Rayo's head around with a snap.

'No it ain't! Mebbe you're dumb enough to fall for that kinda thing, but I'm throwin' down a challenge to this Fancypants.' He pursed his lips and made a smacking sound. 'Sweetie, I can smell your perfume from here — an' I don't like it! *I don' like you!* Now, you gonna draw or do I just shoot your ears off . . . ?'

'Hey!' someone in the crowd yelled. 'The kid's gun's only loaded with blanks!'

That brought a murmur from the men gathered there and a couple of women hurried off with their children.

'No use you goin' for the sheriff, honey,' Rayo called. 'Met him along the trail. *He* wasn't loaded with blanks, but he might just as well've been. Never even got one shot off before I downed him.'

Now Johnny Richards felt cold sweat drenching him. 'I — don't have live ammo.'

Rayo grinned, showing his worn, dirty teeth as he fumbled at his cartridge belt. 'Tha's all right, kid. Figured you'd try to back out by sayin' that. Here.' He tossed six glittering .45 calibre cartridges into the dust at

Johnny's feet. 'Load up — I can wait.'

'Look, put a stop to this!' The man who said the words stepped forward, middle-aged, owner of the general store, as it turned out. 'It's no longer funny and — '

He reeled as Rayo whipped up his gun and slammed him across the head with it, then hit him in the midriff. The crowd gasped as the man stumbled and fell unconscious.

Still holding his Colt, eyes narrowed, Rayo turned back to the pale Johnny Richards. 'Pick 'em up, kid, and load 'em into your Colt, or I'll really shoot your ears off an' spoil your looks . . . '

Johnny hesitated and an old man said quietly, 'I think he means it, kid. He's gunnin' for you. Literally.'

There was nothing else to do, so Johnny, watching Rayo closely, dropped to one knee and gathered the six cartridges. He blew dust from them, drew his Colt — the first time he had worn a big-calibre gun, but one which he had bought for hunting — and Rayo looked like being his first prey.

The automatic actions took over — .22 or .45 calibre, the cartridges still went into a cylinder chamber and the bullets sped from a gun barrel when a man pulled the trigger . . .

Loaded, he holstered the gun and Rayo sneered as he slid his own Colt back into leather. The crowd opened out in a hurry, getting well away.

'You sure you don't just want to make this for fun?' Johnny's voice was raspy and it angered him to have to clear his throat.

'Fun! Hell, you call it fun by billin' yourself all over the southwest as the fastest gun alive? A chicken shit like you usin' a pea-shooter, wearin' a fancy dress cowpoke's outfit, claimin *that!*' Rayo shook his head, stabbed himself in the chest with a reversed thumb. '*I'm* the fastest gun alive an' I aim to prove it to you and this whole lousy town — right — *now!*'

The street reverberated to the crash of gunfire, one shot half a heartbeat behind the other, thick clouds of gunsmoke momentarily hiding the two gunfighters.

Then one crumpled and sprawled in the dust.

4

The Shaping of Rogue

'He was the first man I killed,' Martin Sands told Sheriff Vince Starrett.

'But not the last — I know you now. 'Rogue' Richards. Your uncle may've given you that nickname, but I've heard others say you earned it because you reminded them of one of those rogue stallions you always find in any bunch of horses — sleek and clean-looking on the outside, but with a streak of mean inside a mile wide.'

Sands held the man's smug gaze and said flatly, 'I didn't go looking for gunfights.'

Starrett gave a short derisive laugh. 'Well, a devil of a lot of them found you, as I recall.'

'I guess that's how most folk see it.'

'Is there any other way?'

'Damn right.'

'Don't cuss in my office, if you don't mind.'

'The 'fastest gun' tag stuck to me, thanks to some over-zealous reporter building up Roya who claimed that he was the fastest gun alive — and I beat him. Hell, I was barely seventeen!'

'Then you've had a long association with killing.'

'Forced into it, but I admit after a while I didn't even bother trying to dodge the challenges. Get it over and done with, was how I thought. If it meant I lost the title . . . ' He shrugged and spread his hands.

The sheriff's long fingers with very clean nails, tapped briefly against the desk. 'So — that's how you got started on your gunfighting career.'

Suddenly, Martin Sands leaned forward and crushed out the burning cheroot against the polished edge of the desk. The lawman was outraged, but checked abruptly as he began to rise out of his chair — a gun muzzle was pointing at him, just above where the cheroot ash was still smoking.

'I didn't make a career of gunfighting, Vince.'

'Not — not what your reputation would suggest.' He eased back into the chair, but his knuckles where white where he gripped the wooden arms. He didn't relax until Sands holstered his Colt, taking his time about it. 'You are — very fast!'

'Where I could, I walked away, but not always.'

'I'd say 'always' — at least, looking at it in the light that you were the only one to walk away.'

'What would you rather I'd done, Vince? Stood there and let some boozy glory-hunter shoot me down?'

Starrett sighed. 'I suppose there was little choice. But where did 'Martin Sands' come from? Were you trying to dodge the 'Rogue Richards' reputation by changing your name?'

'Different story, Vince.' The words were clipped, the wide mouth set in a hard line.

The sheriff spread his hands. 'I've got time — and it's too early to expect Joanna to be recovered from the anaesthetic.' Sands stood up. 'Sit down, Martin! I'll call you that for now — I understand your restlessness. Bear with me, I need to get your background — and it'll help keep your mind off your troubles, for a time at least, by talking.'

He reached suddenly into a desk drawer and brought out a bottle of bourbon. He smiled faintly at the surprise on Sands' face. 'I don't drink, Martin, but I have nothing against the habit — in moderation. Would you care to imbibe?'

'I could sure use a belt,' Sands admitted and the sheriff produced a glass and filled it.

Sands drank twice, rolling the whiskey around his mouth before swallowing. 'Hits the spot. Thanks, Vince. I dunno why you want to know about me. We never had much to do with each other, you and me.'

'I'm curious, but I think you're in some kind of trouble, and I'd like to help — really. In my capacity as sheriff, or — as plain Vince Starrett'

'The Church Deacon? Look, Vince, I'm obliged for your interest but I'm no church-goer.'

'Which is your loss — and your own decision. But, speaking as sheriff, I'd like to know why the name change — it tends to make one think of you hiding from something — or someone — rather desperately.'

Sands eyed the bottle, hesitated, and, at a nod from Starrett, filled the shotglass and drank slowly.

As he set it down, empty, he said, 'All right, Vince — but I'll tell you now, it's nothing you're going to expect, and there won't be much you can check to see if I'm telling the truth or not.'

Vince lifted a hand. 'I don't pre-judge such things, Martin — I always mull them over before making a decision, But first I have to hear — your — story!'

Sands smiled thinly at the impatience creeping into the sheriff's voice, deliberately took his time making himself comfortable in his chair.

'I'll cut a few corners, things you won't need the details of. For a start, my father and both uncles died during the first two years after I quit the circus: Pa's horse stumbled and he went over a cliff, Uncle Ben was killed in a brawl when he tried to help the young son of a friend and Uncle Wes died in bed, of fever. By that time, I was trying to make my own way . . . '

'As a gunfighter?'

'No! I hired out to a trail herd as wrangler and bronc-buster and followed the cattle trails for years doing that job.'

'You must've run into someone who knew your reputation.'

'You keep interruptin' we'll be here till sundown. All right, I had a few gunfights, but nothing out of the ordinary. Sometimes the boys'd give me more drinks than I really wanted and I'd demonstrate some trick shooting.

When word got around about that, I had the occasional ... challenge — always some fool just had to find out if I was really that fast dodging lead. Once a feller who wouldn't take no for an answer turned out to be the son of the local sheriff and I had to run — the old man put a price on my head.'

Vince looked at him sharply. 'Still there?'

'Long forgotten — I went up to Montana and Wyoming, started trappin' and breaking mustangs, eventually got so much work I needed help — so I took a partner.' He glanced at the lawman. 'Feller named Jason Craig.'

'Ah! Joanna's unfortunate brother! Now I see we are getting into more current times — as you seem to have very carefully skipped several years!'

Sands remained silent for a long time. 'Use your imagination if you want 'em filled in.'

'Oh, I will. But, go on — you took Jason Craig as a partner in your mustang business ... '

* * *

He was a good-looking young ranny, Jason Craig. Girlish eyes, soft-looking skin and curly black hair. His mouth looked kind of soft, too, and seemed to be attractive to women of all ages.

But Jason was a hard worker, good with horses and most animals, wild or tamed: at one time he had a wolf coming in regularly for his supper — well-gnawed chop bones and any gravy-soaked bread crusts on offer. A drifter they fed at their camp-fire took note and while Jason and John Richards were out trapping horses, managed to entice the always hungry wolf to within range of his six-gun.

By the time the mustangers reached the camp in order to investigate the gunshots, the wolf was dead and skinned.

It was Jason who rode along the drifter's trail and returned with the wolf skin tied behind his saddle. He never said what had happened and had a jacket made out of the hide.

'Kinda small, ain't it,' opined Richards when Jason showed him the finished garment.

'Oh, not for me — for my sister Joanna. She's got a birthday comin' up soon. Figured I might ride down to Laramie and give it to her.' He paused. 'We could take what hosses we've already busted, Johnny, and sell 'em — and you could meet her.'

Richards thought about it and agreed. 'We've got enough to make a decent stake. Then we can try up along the Milk River before winter sets in.'

So it was arranged and Johnny Richards met Joanna. Like most men he was dazzled by her beauty and was surprised when she agreed to let him take her to a settlers' dance the following Saturday night.

Over breakfast next morning, Joanna still asleep, Jason looked at his quiet partner over the rim of his coffee cup. 'Noticed you din' lose any time smoochin' up to Jo last night.'

Richards was annoyed to feel his face

flush. 'Well — it was — kind of mutual.'

'Noticed that, too.' Jason laughed suddenly. 'Don't look so worried! Jo's old enough to know her own mind — I ain't gonna come down on you like a watchdog kid brother . . . ! Hell, it'd pleasure me considerable to see you two hitch up.'

'Now wait a minute! You're getting carried away, Jace!'

Jason merely smiled: he had been around enough to know the signs. Here was a couple, altar-bound if ever he had seen two people in love at first sight.

The way Johnny Richards found reasons not to go back into the wilds and start trapping wild horses, with winter approaching, only confirmed Jace's contention.

Then Johnny started hanging around the land agency, checking out land available for settlement — it would have to be on prove-up, as he didn't have enough money to buy any real acreage.

So they went back to trapping horses as soon as the snows eased and found they had rivals in two or three other mustangers' groups aiming to cash in while the horses were still using the graze in the foothills. Once the snows thawed, they would follow the receding snowline back up into the ranges proper.

Richards returned to camp early one evening and had wondered why he hadn't smelled smoke or cooking on the way up the draw — until he found Jason beaten bloody and dumped at the edge of the creek. Sign told him he had been dragged across and thrown into the shallows. It was lucky he hadn't drowned. Somehow he had managed to work his upper body back enough to keep his face out of the ice-cold water.

'Who was it?' Richards asked after he had got Jace into some dry blankets and patched up some of his cuts and bruises. The young ranny had trouble moving: they had worked over his ribs real good and it would be at least a week until he could ride.

'McKenna's bunch,' Jason gasped.

'Mack himself — with them — bro-brothers . . . '

'The Keatons?' It was an unnecessary question: Mel and Garner Keaton were not only McKenna's pards, they were his trouble-shooters and had bullied a couple of other outfits until they finally quit the lucrative area, even though there were plenty of horses to support at least four or five gangs of mustangers.

Now it seemed they aimed to drive off Richards and Craig, too . . . and take what stock they had already gathered.

Jason watched as Johnny Richards sat on a log and began cleaning his Colt, his rifle propped beside him, awaiting its turn for the same attentions — and close to hand should McKenna return.

'Wish you'd — wait, I'll be — up an' about — in a few days.'

'You won't. And you don't let sidewinders like McKenna 'wait'. You go retaliate pronto, or you lose.'

'But — there are three of them! And they're all experienced gunfighters,

68

Johnny! I know you're fast, of course, and you did down that cocky kid up in Crescent Creek, but these sons of bitches've got real bloody hands!'

'Time they had 'em washed, then.'

Jason was still pleading with him to wait until he could ride, too: after all, he was the one got beaten up. But Richards merely saddled his big sorrel, checked the Colt one more time and made sure the Winchester was set firm in its scabbard.

'Be back by sundown, but don't worry about supper — I'll cook us up somethin'.'

'Judas! I wish I had your confidence!' Jason murmured quietly as he tried to ease into a more comfortable position in his bedroll and his pard dropped over the crest of the hogback, lifting his left hand slightly in a wave.

'Christ, I hope that ain't the Last Farewell!' Jason said aloud . . .

* * *

Johnny Richards recognized the bunch of ten half-broken horses he and Jason had been working. They were in a newly-built corral on the slope of McKenna's camp and he tightened his lips as he saw the bloody flanks and other welts and marks from the Keatons' rough handling.

The three men, McKenna and the Keatons, were hunkered down around the cooking fire, making an early supper it seemed. Garner Keaton, wide and heavy but none too tall, reached for the coffee pot — but snatched his hand back as if a snake had struck at it when the pot leapt into the air, spraying hot black coffee through a sudden bullet hole.

The crack of the rifle reached his ears as he threw himself backwards, knocking his brother off the log as the fire sizzled and half the coals were extinguished.

McKenna himself, a tough, long-muscled horse thief from way back, rolled off his log seat, dragging his Colt as he did so. Mel Keaton was on his knees now, six-gun out, edge of his left hand chopping at the hammer.

The shots were wild but forced Richards to duck and dodge. Garner, face burned from the splashing coffee and so in a right killing mood, roared, reared to his feet and snatched up his shotgun, whirling and shooting with blurring speed.

Johnny Richards rolled swiftly as buckshot churned the earth beside him, stones and twigs scattering. He lost his rifle, followed through automatically with a shoulder-roll as he had used in his circus act. As he bounced to his knees, his Colt triggered twice. Garner, startled by the move, fired the second barrel of his shotgun as Johnny's bullets slammed home and twisted him violently, towards his brother. The charge of buckshot brought a scream from Mel and he fell, one arm dangling, bloody, flesh shredded. McKenna was running for his horse and Richards went after him. McKenna, long experienced in gunfights, dived over a log and twisted in a body-wrenching move, before he hit the ground, his body coming round with the hand that held his six-gun resting on the log.

Richards was stumbling on the slope and just straightening as McKenna bared his teeth in anticipation of a kill. 'You ain't fast enough this time, mister!'

Wrong! Even as the hammer fell, Johnny's gun snapped into line and bucked against his wrist. McKenna was flung back a yard, the top of his head spinning away like a rag mop.

Breathing hard, Johnny walked across to the screaming Mel Keaton. 'Your own brother's done for you, Mel.'

Mel's contorted face stared up at him. He raised his voice but it was very weak. 'Garn! Get this — sonuver! He's — '

'Too late, Mel. He's gone. Go say 'howdy' to him.'

The last bullet in Johnny's Colt put an end to McKenna's thieving outfit.

5

Diamond H

Jason Craig recovered more quickly than Richards expected and, he suspected, more quickly than Jace himself expected, too.

'What we gonna do with them hosses you found corralled back in the woods, Johnny? They're already branded — range stock that's been stole, I reckon.'

'Yeah — only thing to do is find out where this Diamond H is and return 'em.'

Jason Craig nodded, but, it seemed to Richards, somewhat reluctantly.

'That's the right thing, Jace,' Johnny told him and the younger man nodded jerkily, smiled.

'Yeah — just had a little dream about gettin' a quick start to a small ranch . . . OK. I think I can find this Diamond H. I rode with a feller used to work there and he talked about it some.'

So they drove the bunch of branded horses for two days and, in the distance, saw a vast sprawl of ranch buildings on grassy slopes that swept down to a big river.

'That'd be the Rattlesnake,' allowed Jace. 'Tributary of the Sweetwater. So that has to be Diamond H.'

Richards had his hands folded on the saddlehorn and had risen slightly in the stirrups to get a better look. 'Man! Now that, is what I call a *ranch!* Look at the cattle! Like a river, so many strung out across all that grass. I've counted seven riders so far.'

Jace nodded. 'Yeah, think that feller said they ran to mebbe twenty-plus hands, even in the winter.'

'They'd need 'em. OK, let's get these broncs back where they belong . . . '

* * *

Three minutes later they were dodging lead as three rifle shots cracked from

74

the rim of a ledge on the slope to their left. The horses veered away but not far, no doubt feeling safe enough on their home range. But even as Johnny's rifle came up to his shoulder a voice called from the rim.

'We got three guns on you and the shootin'll bring in a half-dozen more! You boys'd best stay put and get your stories straight!'

Both Richards and Jason lifted their hands out to the side — empty.

'We're bringin' back your horses!' Johnny called. 'Had a run-in with McKenna and the Keatons after they stole some of our stock — found yours corralled back in the brush.'

There was a brief silence, then a different voice, tougher, steel-edged, said, 'You tangled with McKenna and the Keaton brothers — and you're still ridin'?'

'And bringing back your broncs,' Johnny Richards added. 'McKenna and the Keatons won't bother you again.'

Another short silence, and then riders began to appear from two different directions, attracted by the gunfire, just as the man on the rim had said. They were all armed, and formed a small crescent in front of Richards and Craig. One rode to look at the bunch of horses that were grazing now.

'Our broncs, all right, Case! Had some rough handlin' but seem mostly OK.'

'All right, bring 'em along. We'll take 'em to the home range and let Linus decide.'

'They ain't nesters, Case,' the rider who had checked the herd said.

'I don't care if they're Mormons! Bring 'em in — and take their guns.'

'No.'

The men all looked sharply at Johnny Richards as he spoke.

'You say what?' snapped the rider, and the other two tightened their grips on the rifles.

'We keep our guns.'

'Not if Case says different.'

'And I do!' the man on the rim called down.

Richards could see him now as he stood with one hip cocked, rifle butt braced, holding it with the barrel slanting towards Richards and Craig.

'We're doin' you a favour, Case,' Johnny said. 'We didn't have to bring your horses back.'

'You showed good sense there.'

'Don't seem that way — you're actin' kinda peppery, ain't you?'

Case started to lift his rifle towards his shoulder and then changed his mind. 'Aaah — just keep your hands on the reins and don't make any fast moves. Jim, you and Andy bring the herd in — Mike, ride behind our visitors. I'll join you when you pass the ledge here.'

'Right, Case.'

'Suit you gents?' Case asked sardonically.

'For the moment.'

'You damn sassy for a man under so many guns, feller!'

'Only because I know I could shoot you all out of your saddles before you could pull the trigger.'

A wave of silence and then loud guffaws.

'Hell, Case,' the rider called Jim said, barely able to keep from laughing. 'We got us a coupla comedians here!'

'See how funny they feel when they meet Linus.'

★ ★ ★

Linus Hammond was a bulky man, tanned, clean shaven, thick hair held in place with a little pomade and water. He removed his pince-nez spectacles as he sat at his desk, set down his pen on the tally book he had been checking and leaned back in his chair. He ran a cool, probing gaze over the horse-breakers and spoke to Case Mannering, his foreman, who stood by, hat pushed to the back of his head, revealing dark, sweaty curls. 'Who are they?'

Case jerked his head. 'Tell Mr Hammond your names.'

Richards did so and Hammond studied Jason Craig with his bruises and cuts. 'What happened to you?'

'McKenna and the Keaton brothers.'

The rancher's gaze flicked to Richards. 'You went after those three — alone?'

'Jace was in no condition to ride.'

Hammond's face remained expressionless except for a slight frown. 'I have an impression I've seen or heard of you.'

'If you ever went to a performance of Fraley's Frontier Circus you would've seen me.'

The rancher though and snapped his fingers. 'Yeah! The trick shooter! Hell, you were good. That training must've stood you pretty well on the gun trail.'

'I never started on any gun trail. Idiots kept challenging me until I had to draw or die.'

'Uh-huhh. I've heard from time to time. Case, we could use a couple extra men, couldn't we?'

Case Mannering blinked, obviously taken by surprise at the query. 'We-ell, we don't acshully *need* extra men, boss, but — '

'We do, 'cause I'm thinking I see a way to fix that quarter-section as a buffer between Diamond H and those goddamn nesters.'

Richards and Craig waited, faces carefully blank.

'You two know horses, right? Well, McKenna won't be the last hoss rustler you come across in this country. Too wide open for the law to nail down all the outlaws and they have pretty much a free rein. How'd you like it if I hired you to break-in what horses you've got and any more you can trap and deliver to Diamond H? Guaranteed sale.'

Craig and Richards exchanged glances. *A regular income, grub and a bed — it meant they could save. And Johnny needed to save so he could guarantee Joanna a secure married life: their relationship had reached that stage by now . . .*

'Jace . . . ?'

'OK by me.'

Richards nodded and thanked Hammond.

'Case, take young Jace down to the

80

bunkhouse and get him set. I need a few words with Johnny here.'

Jace hesitated but Richards nodded and Case Mannering led the young horse-breaker out.

'Sit down, Johnny. You a man who likes a snort?'

'Now and again.'

'You'll like this snort — imported from Scotland, aged twelve years in oak.'

'Mouth's watering already.'

They had two drinks, Richards earning a frown of disapproval from Hammond when he tossed the first one down — as was usual with frontier rotgut.

'Jesus, man! Don't waste it! *Sip* it! Get the full flavour.'

Drinking that way was sure an improvement. 'Never had anythin' as smooth and sweet as that before,' allowed Richards.

'We'll have another soon — maybe to celebrate.'

'Celebrate what?' asked Johnny, puzzled.

'There's a quarter-section up for

81

grabs right on my northwest line — under prove-up, of course. I've so far managed to — discourage — some nesters who have their goddamn farms and hog wallows just round the bend of the river from this land I'm talking about.'

''Discouraged' . . . ?'

Hammond shrugged big shoulders. 'Good a word as any. Had to spread a little — er — goodwill — in the right places, if you know what I mean.'

'Like the land agency.'

'Yeah, but gotta be careful there. They're talking about making the Territory a State and everything has to be clean and smooth. *I* can't apply for the land because I already own so much and they know all my men so I can't even put one of them in to claim the six months prove-up. But they dunno you.'

'If I come to work for you they will.'

'We-ell, let's say young Jace can work for me as a wrangler. You'll still be in my pay but no one needs to know about that. You can put in your claim on that land and get it in your name.'

'You want me to prove up by the deadline?'

'That's right. I'll pay you top hand's wages while you're doing it, supply any materials you need — even lend you a couple of my hands to help out.' He lifted a hand as Johnny made to speak. 'Don't worry, I can do all that and the agency will turn a blind eye — if anything should go wrong, they'll just say they had no idea you were really stooging for Diamond H.' He waited but Richards said nothing. 'Once you've proved up, that land's yours and you can sell to whoever you like.'

He smiled crookedly, shoulders hunched a little, putting some effort into his unspoken offer.

'You'll buy the land off me when I've proved up?'

'Top price, you've got my word on it . . . Is it a deal?'

With that much money guaranteed, he and Joanna could be off to a mighty fine start in their marriage — it only meant waiting another six months and without Hammond's deal, it could — would — be a hell of a lot longer . . .

'How about another slug of that fine old Scotch?'

Hammond's gaze was careful. 'Are we celebrating a deal . . . ?'

'We are.' Johnny rose and offered his hand across the desk.

The rancher stood, beaming as they shook, and then reached for the bottle.

★   ★   ★

'What a helluva piece of luck, Johnny!'

Jason Craig was genuinely pleased when Richards told him of the deal he had made. They were sitting on the top rail of one of the corrals, smoking, after a fine supper in the bunkhouse. A few stars were just beginning to shine.

'Yeah — can't believe it, Jace. You'll be OK, too. They seem a decent enough bunch, the cowhands.'

Jason's face straightened a little. 'Yeah — I guess.'

'What's wrong . . . ?'

'Well, nothin' really — 'cept I heard a couple talkin': they'd just come in from out-riding the southern range, had been there a few days it seems, collectin' strays, and one had some buckshot in one arm. His pard was pickin' it out, pellet by pellet. Din' seem too serious but . . . '

'What happened?' Richards was sobering fast.

'From what I gather they were shot at by some nesters while they were driving some Diamond H steers across the nester's land and kinda lettin' 'em wander into his crop gardens.'

Richards swore. 'Goddamnit! Hammond never gave any hint there was that kinda trouble between him and the nesters! I figured things would be tense: they always are with cattlemen and settlers, but — '

'Aw, might've just been the outriders themselves — they look pretty tough — but if you're gonna be workin' land butting-up against the farmers, just be careful, Johnny, huh? You know, you might be bein' — used.'

Richards had the same idea — and it didn't make him happy . . .

Not a man to sit and fret over such things, Johnny Richards went to see Hammond the next day after he had helped Jace bring down their collection of mustangs. They would finish breaking them in on the ranch, and then sell them to Linus Hammond.

The rancher's face stayed unsmiling and grim-jawed as Richards told him Jason's story. He waved a big hand.

'Collis and Pierce — couple of hardcases but you need a few men like that scattered among your cowhands in this country, Johnny. They're a mite provocative, but both had families who suffered when nesters and sheepherders moved into their valley up in Montana, crowded out the small ranchers. I'll have a word with 'em.'

'They seemed to think you'd approve of what they did.'

Hammond's eyes narrowed. 'Why

wouldn't I? I've got no sympathy for nesters taking over this basin — and that's what they'll do if we don't keep 'em in check. I like to keep the peace and do most things by the book — occasionally I work around it, I admit. But don't worry. You won't be involved in anything like that.'

'No — I won't,' Johnny answered flatly.

Hammond pursed his lips thoughtfully as Richards stood and left abruptly.

★   ★   ★

The land was filed in Richards' name within the week. Hammond was well pleased, and it showed the way he stood all his cowhands to a night on the town in nearby Dancing Tree.

Whatever arrangements he made with the land agent were never made known publicly. He sent some men across to clear ground as a site for the cabin he wanted Richards to build and

87

have it ready for when he wanted to move in.

Meantime, Johnny gave Jason a hand to finish breaking in the horses they had brought down from their campsite. True to his word, Linus Hammond bought the lot when they had finished and the money was paid into a bank account opened in Richards' and Craig's names.

They had always split fifty-fifty and there was no reason to change now.

'If you see Joanna, don't tell her the full deal — just that we're working for steady wages on Diamond H.'

Jason grinned. 'You aim to surprise her, huh?'

'This is only a start, Jace — the big deal will be when I prove up and Linus buys me out.' He couldn't keep from grinning. '*Damn!* I can hardly wait to see her face!'

But that pleasure was six months away: after a successful prove-up.

*   *   *

Two months later Richards had a visit from the nesters.

There were a few of Hammond's cattle on the quarter-section, grazing on the grass near the river, helping keep the land free of too much vegetation while Johnny Richards worked on his cabin.

It was coming along fine — Jace and two other Diamond H hands had helped him fell and trim the trees and when he was ready, start placing the logs for the walls. But he was working alone the day he heard a cow's plaintive bawling — much closer than where he'd set the cattle grazing.

Stripped to the waist, he straightened with a small grunt of effort and wiped sweat from his face with a kerchief. There were riders coming up from the river — and they were driving three cows.

Johnny stepped to the nearby tree where his six-gun rig was hanging and he had it buckled on and was smoking a cigarette when the riders arrived. *Three* men *and a boy about fourteen or fifteen.*

They carried guns but their Colts were in their holsters and the rifles in the saddle scabbards. Their clothes were roughly patched and not too clean: *No womenfolk to care for them* . . . Richards decided.

The grey-haired rider with the spade beard touched a hand to his ratty-looking hat brim. 'Name's Chad Marchant — these here are my brothers, Sam with the big beak, Saul the other. Boy on the end is my son, Cal.'

Johnny gave them the once-over, thinking, *Just like my own deal, father, uncles . . . no womenfolk . . .*

He walked across, reached up to each, offering his hand. They seemed a mite surprised but shook briefly, Sam and Saul more leery than Chad. The boy just nodded and gave a quick squeeze of Johnny's fingers that wouldn't have squashed a fly. 'I'm John Richards, proving up. See you brought back a couple of my cows.'

The men stiffened and Johnny Richards frowned. Saul said, 'So you admit they're yours.'

There was belligerence there and for a moment Johnny felt glad he had strapped on his Colt.

'Well, not actually *mine*. They belong to Linus Hammond as you can see by the brand. He's letting me graze them to help keep down the vegetation while I build my cabin.'

'Friend of yours, Linus Hammond?' asked Chad slowly.

'Seems friendly enough, helping me out so I can make the deadline.'

Sam spat. 'What we figured! You're stoogin' for Hammond, gonna prove up and sell out to him! Give him this piece of land so he can go right ahead with his plans to starve us out!'

'Slow down, Sam,' Chad said quietly, but his face was harder now as he regarded Richards. 'Is that how it is?'

'The land's filed in my name. I aim to build a cabin here, stock the range with the necessary number of cattle to qualify for ownership.'

They waited and when he said no more, Chad asked curtly, 'And . . . ?'

'Well, it'll be mine to do with what I want.'

'Like sell to Hammond!'

'It'd have to be a damn good offer.' Richards gave a tentative grin but saw that wasn't going to soften the attitude of the nesters.

'Yeah! Worked out already, I reckon!' Saul was the short-tempered one it seemed and he actually started to swing down, only stopped when Chad snapped at him harshly.

The boy licked his lips, looking a little worried as he sensed more trouble brewing.

'We came to return your cows. They seemed to have wandered on to our land — managed to knock down the fence we'd built around our gardens.'

Richards stiffened. 'They're not supposed to be anywhere near your land.'

'I just told you what happened — I thought it was you drove them on to that pocket but I see your shirt hanging up there and it's blue — feller who brought the cows wore a green shirt, forkin' a big paint, but he wasn't close enough for me to see his face.'

'I don't have anyone working for me right now — and I don't own a green shirt. And I ride a sorrel.'

'He's just a Good Samaritan, huh?' Saul asked. 'Seen you were busy and brought in them cows and hazed 'em agin our fence till it gave way. Just right an' convenient for you!'

Johnny's gaze was brittle. 'That's a lie, mister.'

The boy, Cal, sucked in his breath sharply and sat up straighter in the saddle, looking quickly at his uncle to see how he would take it.

Saul's lips peeled back from broken teeth and he jammed home the spurs, leaping his mount forward with a sudden yell. 'Ya-haaaah!'

Richards jumped aside but not fast enough to miss the boot that Saul kicked free of his stirrup and planted viciously against his shoulder. Johnny went sprawling and Saul, ignoring a yell from Chad, urged his mount forwards, trying to ride over Richards.

Johnny rolled and scrabbled and Saul worked reins and spurs and used his body weight, dogging Richards' every move, trying to drive him back against a stack of logs awaiting bark-peeling. Johnny slipped and a hoof skidded off his hip and he figured that was enough. He rose from the ground like he was propelled by a spring and saw the stark surprise on Saul's stubbled face as he lifted up almost level with the man's head.

Saul hauled rein and reared back in the saddle, but Johnny's Colt swung up and slammed him across the side of his head, knocking him out of leather. As he dropped back, Richards stumbled and crouched, even as Sam spurred his mount towards him, dragging at his six-gun which was rammed into his belt.

Johnny triggered into the ground, his bullet landing between the forefeet of

Sam's mount. It shied and whinnied and Sam half-fell off the horse. Richards grabbed him and heaved him to the ground, rounding on Chad who was pulling his revolver now — but halted as Johnny's hammer cocked.

'Stay put! You, too, boy.'

Cal whipped his hand away from his rifle stock and let it fall back into the scabbard.

'So!' Chad said a little breathlessly. 'Hammond's hiring gun fighters now!'

'No — I'm here to prove up on this land, just like I told you. Then I'll sell it, most likely to Hammond, but not necessarily. But that's my business — you nesters want to get along with folk, you need to put a rein on your tempers.'

He gestured to the two brothers, helping each other up now, looking cross-eyed, no doubt their ears ringing wildly.

'You got the quick moves of a gunfighter,' Chad said stubbornly. 'But I admit mebbe Sam and Saul were a mite edgy. We been hassled a'plenty since we come here, like we got no right to make what we want of land we bought or are payin' for.'

'Mister, you come into the middle of established cattle country and start planting crops and bring in hogs and milkin' cows, you're *gonna* get hassled. Stands to reason.'

'We know that!' growled Saul, holding a grubby rag to the bleeding wound above his right eye where Richards' gun barrel had hit him. 'We came here to make our farms and work 'em. We din' need to build fences till Diamond H cows started 'wanderin' ' — least that's what Hammond called it! Stomping down our crops an' seedlings. Hell, that's our livelihood! Just like fattenin' cows is yours!'

'Saul's right,' Chad said. 'And we don't have to take all the hassles lyin' down . . . '

Richards looked at them one by one, including the boy, holding his Colt loosely down at his side, but knowing they weren't going to try anything now they'd seen him in action.

'Don't blame you. But while I'm provin' up here you won't get hassled by me. Now that's my word on it, and I don't give it lightly.'

The Marchants looked at each other, plainly puzzled but Chad eventually said, clearing his throat, 'Sounds like a fair deal. Reckon we'll take you at your word — Richards, is it?'

'Johnny Richards.' He holstered his gun and lifted his right hand again. 'You want to start over . . . ?'

The boy, Cal, was the first to shake it.

6

Buck-Jump

They came pretty close to being friends as the weeks passed, the nesters and Richards, and Hammond didn't like it.

'I'm paying you to satisfy prove-up requirements with this land,' he snapped on one of his visits to the cabin site.

It was looking good, all the walls up, windows cut and shuttered, the roof frame ready to take shingles, which Richards was laboriously cutting, knee deep in the pile of the sharp-smelling cedar shakes when Hammond rode in with Case Mannering. He straightened stiffly, dropped the tools and reached for the rag he kept for wiping sweat from his now tanned torso.

'You can see the progress. Reckon if I made enemies outta the Marchants and other nesters, there wouldn't be much more than the lower walls built.'

'I heard they been bringing you grub.'

'Haunch of smoked pork, mighty fine eating.'

'Bud Holbrook, one of my top hands, said you wouldn't let him drive a bunch of cows across,' Case accused. 'To kinda let wander on the Marchants' place later on.'

'That's right — didn't see any sense in rilin'-up the nesters when they're not bothering anyone.'

'They bother me, damn you!' snapped Hammond. He lifted a hand off his saddle horn and shook a stiffened finger towards Richards who was rolling a cigarette. 'You give no mind to good relations with them nesters, specially the Marchants. They been a thorn in my side for a long time — I figured settin' you up here was the answer to my probelms. Now I'm wondering if I was wrong.'

Richards cupped a hand around the match flame. 'I don't see your problem, Linus — I'll still make prove-up on time and I'll sell to you . . . nothin's changed.'

Hammond glared. 'Mebbe you get too friendly with the Marchants you won't want to sell to me.'

Johnny Richards drew deeply on his cigarette and exhaled a long bluish plume before answering. 'You mean if there's any truth in Chad Marchant's suspicion you're gonna dam the river here and control his main water supply, if not cut it off altogether?'

Hammond swore. 'So, the son of a bitch's thinking along those lines!'

'When he first mentioned it, I took time to check the river and how it flows. I reckon he's got cause to at least worry about it happening. Here's a perfect position to cut the water, not just to him, but the nesters' end of the valley. A man felt mean enough, he could starve out the whole shebang. But he needs this land to do it.'

'And you wouldn't like that?'

Johnny gave him a steady look, dragged it out until he saw Hammond frown in annoyance and get ready to speak. Then he said, 'Not if I was a nester.'

Hammond swallowed whatever he was going to say, smiled slowly and then laughed. 'Me, neither! You're a cattleman at heart then, Johnny?'

'Horses, rather than cows, but you got the right idea. But that makes no nevermind, as my old man used to say. What you're planning is gonna start a damn range war.'

'The nesters won't have a range to worry about because there won't be any water.'

'Linus, you're a damn hard man, but you could be in for a surprise. Only nesters I've met are the Marchants and one of their neighbours — Cattrell — he looks a real hardcase. They'll fight for what they believe is their right — can't blame 'em for that.'

'We know Cattrell,' said Case Mannering, unconsciously rubbing one side of his jaw. 'He's got a reckonin' comin' too.'

Richards sighed. 'OK, so it's out in the open now: all this is aimed at getting rid of the nesters. Now I'm no nester-lover, Linus: they grow food and we buy it and eat it. I don't hate 'em, but what I do hate is being used the way you're usin' me.'

Hammond made a disparaging gesture. 'Aaah — hell, you'll be well paid, you'll be able to marry your woman and live pretty damn good. What's your beef?'

'If you don't savvy now, you never will.'

He just seemed to jerk his arm slightly and suddenly his Colt was in his fist, hammer back, barrel steady.

'What the hell!'

Mannering jumped. 'God, I never even seen him *move!*'

'Ride on out, Linus, and take Case with you. This land's in my name right now and I have a say in who stands on it. You two don't qualify at this moment.'

Hammond's face was dark red. Case

Mannering was slightly pale, he had been shocked by Richards' gun speed and knew he and his boss were a breath away from dying, going by the look on Johnny's face.

'You ungrateful son of a bitch!' Linus finally spat, big chest heaving with choking anger.

'I won't hold you to your promise to buy me out, Linus. Fact is, I quite like this spot and maybe Joanna will, too.' He paused and smiled coldly. 'Get that look off your face! She won't be coming here — or anywhere else you snakes could try to grab her just to get at me. Ride on out. Next time I might shoot on sight.'

'By *God!* Don't think you've heard the last of this, Richards!'

'*I know damn well I haven't,*' Johnny said to himself as he watched them ride away.

It was a good move getting rid of them, but not good enough.

By sunup two days later Jason Craig was dead . . .

Like a lot of his story, Richards/Sands worked out what had happened — and in some cases, how and why — then pieced it all together at a later date.

This is what he told Vince Starrett . . .

Jason was a likeable young ranny and most of the men on Diamond H responded to his youthful enthusiasm and good nature. But there was always the bad apple who, through jealousy or envy or God-knew-what, didn't care for someone like Jason Craig being so popular.

So one morning The Demon turned up in the corrals among the half-broken horses, eyes red and watering and mean as a cougar with toothache. He immediately set about biting and kicking and making sure every mare and stallion there understood he was the new boss.

'How the hell'd that thing get down here?' demanded Jim Gallagher, the straw boss. 'He was s'posed to stay in that box canyon till we knocked some more of the vinegar outta him.'

'He's a hoss knows his own mind, I guess,' spoke up Van Ketchum, one of the bronc-busters on the wrangler team. 'Reckon he musta busted out, made his way down here and jumped the fence to get in amongst the others. Yeah! Looky here! Fresh scrapes across the top rail from his hoofs.'

Gallagher whistled softly. 'Some damn jump! Yeah, there's marks there, all right, though they don't look *quite* like hoof scrapes. He's only wearin' dancin' shoes, not the workers, an' they wouldn't scratch that deep.'

He was referring to the lightweight temporary shoes fitted to horses yet to be fully broken in: they would be replaced with heavier regular shoes once they were considered tame enough for work and command.

'Hell, I've seen him jump boulders up in that canyon, higher'n that! Son of a bitch, had me goin' round in circles one time, tryin' to drop a rope on him, I was so damn dizzy it was like I'd had a week on the redeye.'

Gallagher looked at Ketchum with narrowed eyes, 'Yeah, you been the one to try an' work him all along. You couldn'ta hobbled him proper last night.'

'I damn well did hobble him proper!'

'Well, he's here an' you know him best. You can get him outta there an' take him back.'

'Shoot! I ain't that good. Hey, Jace! You always got lots to say about hosses: you wanna gimme a hand?' He added slyly, 'I could let you try ridin' him — heard you say at breakfast yesterday you wouldn't mind givin' it a go.'

'That's enough!' Gallagher snapped before Jason could answer. 'Jace is pretty good but not good enough to tackle that fugitive from hell.'

'Aw, I wouldn't mind, Jim,' Jason said. ' 'Fact, I been thinkin' of some way of comin' up with some money to help out Johnny and my sis — for when they get married.'

'Ridin' The Demon won't get you

nothin' but a heap of time in the infirmary, Jace,' Gallagher told him.

'No, listen, how about I try to ride him for, say, half a minute. That's like five minutes or more on the usual mustang, an' if I make it, all you rannies pitch in with a dollar each, and I can pass it on to Johnny and Jo.'

Jim Gallagher was a conservative man in his forties and he was shaking his head before Jace had quit speaking. But other hands had come up to get as close a look as they dared at The Demon and a few of them agreed to Jason's suggestion. *It could turn out to be a good show . . .*

'Don't mind kickin' in a buck for Johnny Richards!'

'Yeah, I like Johnny. Wish it was *me* gettin' ready to marry that gal — Er, no offence, Jace! That was meant as a comply-ment.'

'Count me in,' said another. 'I'll pitch in a buck.'

'Me, too — I want to see Jace flyin' through the air like the angel he tries to be!' Ketchum grinned tightly.

There was a discussion and the noise brought more idle cowhands across to put in their two cents' worth — or, in most cases, their dollar's worth: nearly all seemed to think it was a good idea. *If nothing else it would break the boredom of ranch work . . . '*

On the outskirts, surly Van Ketchum lifted an arm as if to blot sweat from his face, but mostly to hide his sly smile.

Jason had walked right into the trap like a fly to a honey jar! Whichever way it went, Jace Craig would be a mighty different man after being in the saddle of The Demon. See how popular the sonuver was then!

The Demon, as it became known, attracted a lot of men, not just the Diamond H crew, but hands from neighbouring ranches, even a bunch of barflies who rode out from Dancing Tree. *Just to see the fun!*

All these men worked with horses every day, and so were able to be critical, but they made Jason nervous.

108

Hell, he had busted plenty of ranch horses but this one would require skill and guts! He hoped that even if he didn't go the full half-minute, some of the men might still toss him a few dollars anyway if he put up a good performnce. They were tough but almost all of them had a little soft spot . . .

The ride was a disaster.

The Demon lived up to his name. He kicked one of the nervous handlers in the chest and men straddling the fence rail heard the ribs go. The laughter quickly died and they jumped down, waving hats and hands and yelling, driving The Demon away from his victim. Or trying to. The big horse lowered its head, charged into the bunched men and scattered them like ninepins, bodies arcing and tumbling and rolling all over the grounds trying to escape those driving hoofs and gnashing teeth.

'Boy, you better call this off!' Jim Gallagher said but Jason, white and swallowing hard, shook his head.

'Can't, Jim — I — I gave my word.'

Gallagher, tight-lipped, nodded: he savvied that, but he sure had his reservations . . .

It took another twenty minutes of chaos and near-disaster and three injured men before Jason, shaking like a straw in the wind now, climbed the rails and mounted the snorting devil held by four sweating cowhands. He only got as far as lifting a leg over the saddle when The Demon cut loose.

It arched its back like a bow drawn to the limit, dropped its belly almost to ground level and with a shrill scream snapped taut. Jason had one hand in the air and the other slipped under the belly rope, trapping it, the strands pinning him by the wrist.

His face contorted but no one heard any sound he may have made: the snorting and whickering horse kicked up clods of earth as big as a man's head, splintered two bottom rails, loosened a post, splayed all four feet, legs stiff as iron, leapt straight up and came down, jarring Jason's spine as if it had been hit with a fourteen pound sledge hammer.

He thought the top of his head was coming off.

His mouth filled with blood and he was vaguely aware that he had bitten through part of his tongue. His eyes were rolling like marbles caught in a rainwater drain. His stomach came up into his throat and one of the yelling spectators afterwards reckoned everything Jace had eaten over the past week was expelled in a scalding, curving stream, sending men jumping from their perches on the rails, running for cover.

Everyone could see the blurred form of Jason working his mouth in some sort of plea for help but no one distinguished any words. His head was snapping back and forth on his neck. His teeth chipped as they crunched together. All his internal organs seemed to be swishing around somewhere in his body-cage, ramming up into his throat, and the world was a spinning blur, jarred frequently as The Demon's legs drove again and again into the ground.

The big sweating body rippled with muscle and tendons and then the horse ran at the corral, scattering men again as they tried to corner it, waving coiled ropes and arms. But nothing short of a mighty strong net was going to stop that four-legged cyclone. It suddenly turned side-on and crushed Jason's leg against the cross rails.

They all heard him scream that time.

The Demon ran along the rails, almost tearing Jason's leg from its socket, turned around and smashed into the fence again, crushing the other leg. Jason was jerking and rocking like a rag doll, mostly held on by the hand trapped beneath the belly rope, barely conscious.

Jim Gallagher reckoned it was enough and did what he had wanted to do from the first few seconds: he picked up his rifle and shot The Demon through the head.

It went down instantly, surprising

everyone: a screaming, four-legged fiend from Hell itself ought to have at least gone into some sort of paroxysm with steam streaming from distended nostrils, and hoofs smashing every man-made item within reach, ripping a trench in the earth itself as it scrabbled in its dying convulsions. That was their picture of how that murderous animal should die.

But no: it simply jerked its head violently, the legs folded as if on weakened hinges, and it flopped on its belly, Jason dangling over the side, blood-streaked, unconscious now. Then The Demon lay on its side, stretched out as if in a peaceful sleep.

Men rushed in to jerk and free Jason but even though he was breathing — screeching, wheezing noises gargling up from his smashed chest into his throat — they knew he wouldn't last long.

He surprised them by clinging to life for a day and a half, then died as the sun rose on the second morning.

* * *

A bashful and shamefaced Jim Gallagher took off his hat and proffered it towards the sobbing Joanna at the graveside: the hat crown was filled with paper money.

'The boys wanted you — to have this, ma'am. It was due Jace, in fact, was why he tried to ride that sonofa — The Demon.'

Joanna looked at the soberfaced Richards and after a hesitation he took the hat from Gallagher. 'Thanks, Jim. And thank the men. We know they mean well.'

Gallagher shuffled away through the mourners and Jo looked at Johnny Richards levelly. 'I could never touch that money, Johnny.'

He nodded. 'I'll give it to the Indian agent for the Reservation, if that's agreeable . . . ?'

She nodded. 'Yes, Jace liked Indians. Got along well with them. He — he got along — well — with everyone.' She

114

looked at him accusingly. 'You should have stopped him!'

He didn't bother explaining he wasn't even there: she would know this. It was just grief bringing out every thought her aching mind could touch. *A brief diversion from her overwhelming grief.*

He handed the money hat to the uncomfortable preacher and held Joanna close . . .

After it was all over, Johnny went looking for the Diamond H men among the mourners at the open-air wake, grabbed Gallagher by the arm.

'How'd that damn killer hoss get loose, Jim?'

'Not sure. He was a mean sonuver, Johnny, didn't wanta be broke, but, well, mebbe Van never hobbled him right.'

He wouldn't look at Richards who prompted: 'Or?'

Gallagher shuffled his feet. 'His eyes didn't look . . . right, somehow. So I checked 'em after I killed him and they were full of grit . . . Looked like sulphur dust.'

'What . . . ?'

'Ketchum's been workin' with the tick bath, stirrin' the sulphur in. I looked at some tracks, too and, well, someone led that Demon down to our corrals in the dark and put him in . . . scratchin' marks in the top rail to make it look like the hoss'd jumped over.'

'He'd need a blindfold to keep him quiet, and if it was an old sulphur bag . . .'

'Johnny, there's no proof but — Van's a mean sonuver and he didn't like Jace, but . . . well, I dunno.'

'Where's Ketchum now?'

'Long gone.'

'Which way?' Richards cut in curtly.

'Uh . . . ?' Gallagher waved a hand vaguely towards the hills. 'That's his country, worked an' lived in it for years. You'll never find him in there.'

But Gallagher was talking to himself. Richards strode swiftly and determinedly towards the hitch rail where his

116

sorrel waited patiently. He mounted with easy speed and spurred away, not even looking towards Joanna's cousin's house as he passed by: she was staying there for a few days. He glimpsed a blur of white at a window, not even sure if it was her. He waved once, anyway.

It took him three and a half days to track down Van Ketchum. Then it wasn't so much that he *tracked* the man to his camp, as it was that Ketchum panicked when he couldn't shake Richards no matter what he did. He picked a narrow ledge halfway up the wall of the canyon where he had made camp and drew a bead on Richards as he rode into sight below.

Johnny's sorrel, weary, picking its way across broken shale, stumbled, and the bullet spurted dust from the brim of his hat, knocking it askew and over one eye. The result was that his instinctive return shot missed Ketchum by a hand-span and made the man over confident.

'Hell! They reckon you can shoot the

pennies off a dead man's eyes without markin' him! My kid brother's a better shot than that one you just made!'

'Wasn't trying,' Richards called back and fired two incredibly fast shots into the overhang of rock where the reflected sun threw Ketchum's shadow. 'But I am now.'

Ketchum yelled in fright as the lead disintegrated and hot blobs stung his neck and ear. He lurched up, hit his head on the overhang and stumbled right to the edge, struggling to bring up his rifle.

'And again!' murmured Johnny as he shot twice more.

Both bullets hammered home, jerked Ketchum's body as if it was being yanked by ropes, and then dropped it over the edge. Ketchum slid and rolled and floundered all the way down the slope, coming to rest a couple of yards from where Richards waited.

★   ★   ★

Linus Hammond himself intercepted Johnny Richards on his ride back. The big rancher folded his hands on the saddlehorn and looked hard at him then flicked his gaze to Ketchum draped over his own horse, arms dangling.

'Looks like I'm short another wrangler.'

'Better off without this one. You can cut my pay for the time I've been away tracking him down.'

Hammond stared a minute then lifted a hand casually. 'We'll see. So you don't mind a manhunt — and a shoot-out, huh?'

'Don't make a habit of it'

The rancher pursed his lips, nodded. 'Good way to be, I s'pose. Bury him anywhere you like, except on Diamond H. See you back at the quarter-section. You and me need to talk.'

The rancher halted briefly, to let Richards ride on by, then swung his mount's head.

'I think you're just the sort of feller I need for a chore I have coming up.'

119

Johnny Richards didn't even look at him. The rancher added, 'It'll pay well. Very well.'

Richards kept on riding, not giving any sign he had heard.

'One other thing — Ketchum's got a kid brother. Kinda on the wild side, got the Ketchum mean streak. He looked up to Van, miserable sonuver though he was.'

Richards waved briefly. 'Thanks for the warning.'

'Keep your gun loose — I'll come see you in the morning.'

Johnny Richards rode around a bend out of sight and Hammond sat his mount while he took out a cheroot and lit up.

Then Case Mannering rode out from between two egg-shaped boulders.

'Tough sonuver,' he opined.

'Yeah. You know where Van's kid brother is?'

Case looked at him sharply. 'Heard he's sparkin' that nester gal they call Rollin' Rosie — Cattrell's wife. Calls the kid in when Cat's out workin' the fields . . . '

Hammond swore and spat, jamming his cheroot back between his thinned lips. 'That blamed idiot! By God, if Cattrell finds out . . . ' He let his voice trail off, looked suddenly thoughtful, then looked squarely at his foreman.

'See that the kid hears about Van — but dress it up some. I mean, it don't *have* to've been Ketchum did the bushwhackin' . . . you know.'

Mannering smiled thinly. 'You mightn't believe it, Linus, but I got a wild imagination.'

7

Lynch Party

Ray Ketchum was barely nineteen and his main interest in life at that age was Rosie Cattrell. She had introduced him to the ultimate delights of a man-woman relationship when he had 'accidentally' come upon her taking her bath in a quiet bend of the creek: he had been spying on her for a few days and this particular day the soft bank — because it had rained during the night — gave way and deposited him no more than a yard from where she had left her clothes.

Sitting waist-deep in the milky water she had been angry at first but an innate recklessness in her — knowing he was one of Hammond's cowhands — made her stand up and smile slowly as his eyes almost popped out of his head . . .

They became regular lovers and she enjoyed the extra 'spice' of knowing she was betraying her husband (who, incidentally, was not much of a husband since a mule deer had gored him below the belt some months earlier).

Van Ketchum soon found out about Ray's liaisons and threatened to knock his teeth out if he persevered. Ray had surprised him by standing up for himself — until now, Van had always been able to bully the boy into doing whatever he wanted. But he happened to catch Van in a pretty good mood — he had recently come from being with a squaw from the reservation — and the older Ketchum had suddenly punched the boy lightly on the shoulder.

'Just don't wear it away. And watch out for Cattrell. He ever finds out, you're dead meat.' Before turning away, Van dug some money from his pocket. 'Here, take this. Dunno any gal who wouldn't be happy with a small present, some kinda trinket, maybe, a bottle of perfume . . . '

Ray grinned. 'You're one *helluva* big brother — big brother!'

'Mebbe because I've got one helluva kid brother. Have fun, Ray. Just take care. If there is any trouble, you come see me. I'll take care of it.'

At that moment, Ray felt the strongest affection he'd ever known for his brother, the man who'd raised him after their parents died. He vowed he would do anything for Van, anything . . .

And when he found out Van had been killed by Johhny Richards — from ambush, Case Mannering had told him — that was all he needed.

He even left a red-faced and angry Rosie sitting up in bed, naked from the waist up, with the sheet pushed down.

'Where the hell d'you think you're goin'?' she demanded, quite breathless.

'I'll be back,' he flung over one shoulder as he stormed out, buckling on his gun rig.

'And maybe you won't find me waitin'!' she called after him angrily, punching the sweaty pillows as he left without another word.

She cursed him roundly, then flopped on to her side and pulled the pillow over her face, starting to sob . . .

'Wondered who bought you that lousy perfume.'

Her body stiffened as the muffled voice reached her. She flipped the pillow away from her face, her heart almost stopping as her husband's figure filled the doorway. He was holding a pitchfork with a broken tine. He had been down in the hay paddock, stacking hay for the coming fall, a long way from the cabin, which was why she had set the signal to let Ray Ketchum know it was safe to come in. But then Case Mannering from Diamond H had arrived, gave the kid some kind of bad news about his brother . . .

'I — I told you, Cy! Millie Brent gave it to me! Someone gave it to her but she didn't like the smell.'

'Me neither. Well, I'll take care of that kid — but I'll take care of you first.'

She screamed as he strode forward, holding the broken fork like a deadly lance, aimed at a spot between her breasts . . .

'That's it! Scream *real* loud — an' bring that kid ridin' back licketty-split! Won't do him no good. *Nor you!*'

He lunged and her scream startled a bunch of multi-coloured parrots in the big cottonwood that shaded the cabin, sending them skywards in a screeching cloud, momentarily blotting out the sun.

★ ★ ★

It was Chad Marchant's boy, Cal, who saw the rider coming first.

The man was using his horse recklessly, holding a rifle in one hand, guiding the animal down the slope of the mountain by his knees and the other hand on the reins.

'Pa! Pa, someone's comin' in like

there's a tribe of Injuns after him!'

Chad Marchant was sorting vegetable seeds into various small groups on a makeshift bench outside his barn. He glanced up, tensed when he saw where his son was pointing. He quickly covered the seeds with a ragged tarp, and wiped his hands down his trousers.

'Looks like Cattrell — Judas! Is he riled!'

Chad hurried across the yard to where Cal stood, waiting for the rider to arrive. 'Boy, go fetch your uncles — I got a bad feelin' about this.'

He gave the lad a push and Cal kept looking back over his shoulder as he hurried to the lower fields where he knew his uncles were working.

By then, Cattrell was skidding his mount to a halt and Chad saw the mad, wild eyes and knew instinctively what had happened: he had caught his wife and that damn fool kid from Diamond H! It was only a matter of time, of course, and now . . .

'Lookin' for that Ketchum kid!'

127

Cattrell called hoarsely. 'He rode over this way.'

'Never showed here, Cat. What's wrong?'

'You know what's wrong! *Everyone* knows what's wrong! Like always, the husband's the last to know! Well, I know now and I'm gonna set things to rights!'

'Easy, Cat! Hell, man, don't go gettin' yourself into trouble over this . . . '

'I'm gonna kill that son of a bitch! Now get outta my way, Chad!'

Marchant grabbed the bridle and held the prancing horse. Cattrell raged and swung his rifle but Chad ducked.

'Wait! Wait up, you fool! You kill anyone from Diamond H and we'll have every cowman this side of the Wind River down on us! We can't risk that, Cat! Look, come up to the cabin and have a snort or two and we'll work somethin' out before you go off half-cocked.'

Cattrell glared down at Marchant. 'Half-cocked or not, she'll never cheat on me again!' As Chad moved uneasily, he sneered. 'An' when I'm through with that kid, before I finish him off, he's gonna be missin' a body part or two!'

'Jesus Christ! You'll get us wiped out, Cat! Now get off that horse and — '

Marchant tried to grab Cattrell's leg and heave him out of the saddle, but the wild man clouted him across the head with the rifle barrel and spurred off as Chad started to fall.

'What the hell!' yelled Saul Marchant as he hurried after Cal across the yard. He began to run. 'Cat! You come back here!'

But Cattrell was racing his mount out of the yard and Cal, alarmed now, tears in his eyes, dropped to one knee beside his father who was semi-conscious, blood running down his face. Chad looked at Saul and the other brother, Sam, as he came running up.

'Get — hosses. Cat's caught Rosie and that — Ketchum — kid. Gonna kill him. Hammond'll burn us out . . . We gotta stop Cat!'

* * *

Case Mannering lowered the field glasses to rest his eyes, knuckled them and blinked, then lifted the glasses again.

Yeah, some kind of action at the Marchants' place. He grinned tightly. *That kid nearly went through the roof when he told him Van had been bushwhacked. Case had kind of hinted it might've been one of the Marchants . . .*

Then 'accidentally' coming across Cattrell stacking hay and asking had he seen Ray Ketchum . . .

He knew by the way Cattrell had looked and answered that the man already suspected what was going on — and Case had just hinted enough before riding off . . .

He would have preferred that Cattrell had killed the kid, but Linus had worked out what to do if that didn't happen . . .

And it hadn't! He stiffened and refocused the field glasses: *Yeah!*

There! Crossing the creek . . . riding like Old Nick himself was after him in his eagerness . . . That kid!

Case could see easily which trail the kid was following. He slid down from his vantage spot atop a boulder and dropped neatly into the saddle of his sturdy paint.

By the time the kid came charging through Powderkeg Gulch, Case Mannering was in position, rifle fore-end resting on a folded kerchief, butt snugged firmly into his shoulder, flesh feeling the sun-warmth of the rifle's cheekpiece.

He let the wild-eyed kid ride by before he fired. The bullet took Ray between the shoulders, half-lifted him out of the saddle. His body fell forwards on to the horse's arched neck and Case shot him again twice. This time the body was slammed from the saddle, hit the ground hard and bounced and rolled.

Case put up the smoking Winchester, hearing the gunfire crackling away through the hills, and climbed down to make sure Ray Ketchum had landed on the Diamond H side of the creek.

He had.

Case glanced up at the distant dust cloud coming from the direction of the Marchants' place.

'Come on in, fellers! We'll be waitin'!'

* * *

John Richards was standing beside a big wooden vice he had made and which held some dressed pine slats. He had a brace-and-bit in his hands as he watched the riders coming, recognizing Hammond and Mannering and four Diamond H cow-hands.

'You hear that shootin'?' called Linus Hammond before he had halted his sweating mount.

Richards frowned and shook his head. 'Been pit-sawing, just started drilling. What's up?'

'Those damn Marchants! They bush-whacked Ray Ketchum, caught him while he was crossing the creek and put three bullets in his back. His horse came out on Diamond H land — we're going after the sonuvers.'

Richards frowned. 'You're going into the nesters' valley?'

'Damn right! I'm gonna nip this in the bud before it gets outta hand.'

'What gets outta hand? Why'd they kill young Ray?'

'Don't really matter, does it?' snapped Mannering. 'They did it — and I saw it! All Marchants: Chad, Sam, Saul, even the boy, Cal.'

It didn't set right with Johnny Richards. He figured Ray Ketchum might come after him seeing as he had killed his brother, but why would the nesters shoot the kid . . . ?

'It's got somethin' to do with young Ray and Rosie Cattrell. But the point is, them nesters done it! They killed one of my men, for whatever reason and it's gotta be set right — *Now!* You leave whatever you're doing and ride along on this, Johnny. You're in it somehow and we'll find out what's going on.'

Richards didn't care for this deal but he figured he had best go along and see what Hammond had in mind. Judging the man's mood now — and that of Mannering and the cowhands — Linus was out for eye-for-an-eye revenge . . .

They crossed the creek, leaving one of the hands to take Ray Ketchum's body back to the main house. *They had shot the kid up, all right — one bullet would have been enough to finish him, but they'd given him two more. It was a cold-blooded murder and Richards felt the anger starting to rise in him . . .*

The Marchants saw the cattlemen coming and wheeled their mounts and headed back towards their cabins, figuring their own land offered more safety than riding on open range with Hammond and his men obviously out for blood.

Of course, all of the Marchants denied shooting Ray Ketchum, or even reaching the creek boundary: they had turned back as soon as they saw the

Diamond H riders coming.

'We saw Mannering talkin' with Ray earlier not far from Cattrell's,' said Saul.

'That's right,' Case Mannering admitted. 'I was tellin' him his brother was dead.' He flicked his gaze towards Richards. 'Had a shoot-out with Johnny there.'

Richards glared, looked at the Marchants and told them how it had come about. They all knew Jason Craig and how The Demon had killed him . . . and Ketchum's mean streak.

Chad looked bleakly at Johnny. 'So you went after Ketchum — one of your own men!'

'Not my man — I don't work for Diamond H, but Jace was a damn good friend of mine.'

'And you bushwhacked Van Ketchum — according to Ray,' Chad said flatly.

'Then he got it wrong — I was the one got bushwhacked. But never mind that. What about shootin' the kid three times in the back?'

'Yeah,' Hammond said not wanting anyone to lose sight of this. 'You stepped over the mark this time, Chad. Murder's a hangin' offence.'

Johnny stiffened right along with the alarmed Marchants.

'The law better decide that, Linus,' he said, gaze hard and steady.

'*I'm* deciding it!' the rancher snapped. 'Right now!'

They were ready for him, figuring he would protest, and he didn't even realize it!

Fast as he was, Johnny Richards wasn't fast enough to dodge the gunbarrel that crashed into his head, swung by one of the cowhands behind him. It crushed in his hat and sent him reeling even as his Colt cleared leather and triggered involuntarily into the ground.

There was a slight melee and the nesters took advantage of it to wheel their mounts and ride up the slope towards their cabins.

'After 'em!' shouted Hammond, and the Diamond H crew spurred after the nesters. Guns blazed but Hammond yelled:

'No shooting! We're gonna show these goddamn nesters that they don't belong in this valley! The Marchants are gonna give 'em a lesson they won't forget!'

They rode after the Marchants, leaving Richards clinging drunkenly to his saddlehorn, blood trickling down from under his hat brim. Semi-conscious, he instinctively dug in the spurs and sent the sorrel up the slope after the others.

By the time he arrived, vision blurred, head throbbing, and barely able to stay on his horse, Hammond's men had the Marchants under their guns by the big barn: the nesters were far more at home with a plough than six-guns and were basically peaceful men.

They'd held their fire too long and now they were going to pay the price.

Richards had managed to hold on to his six-gun during his ride and now he lifted it, triggered a shot into the air, bringing the cowboys spinning around, but making no hostile moves with his smoking gun covering them.

He blinked, seeing the ropes held in the hands of the cowboys. Hammond glared.

'Get out of here, Johnny! This is Diamond H business now,' Hammond snapped.

'It's murder and you know it! Drop your ropes — there'll be no lynching.'

'Wrong!' said Case Mannering who was slightly behind Johnny. He fired his Colt and the bullet whipped the hat off Richards, ploughed alongside his ear and sent him tumbling from the saddle to sprawl on his side, gun lost, face streaked with blood.

'Don't need to worry about him any more, Linus,' Case said with a crooked grin. 'Just another victim of them mean ol' nesters, eh? What next?'

'You know what comes next.'

Mannering nodded slowly. 'All of 'em?'

'Yeah, hang 'em all. The whole Marchant clan — three men — and the boy! Now get it done!'

And that was what Johnny Richards saw when he first started to rally from his unconsciousness.

Four hanging from the heavy branch of the cottonwood, above the smoking ashes that were all that was left of the barn.

'Bastards done a first class job, din' they?'

He wasn't sure whether he had said that out loud or if — someone else . . . He tried to turn his head but it was too much for him.

Then, once more, he plunged into oblivion.

8

Cold Sweat

The burning barn had been seen by other ranchers and farmers in the valley and riders began arriving in small bunches, most horrified, grimly regarding the sight of the four lynched Marchants, bodies turning slowly on the ropes.

'By God! This ain't good,' allowed one of Hammond's neighbours, Fletcher of Broken F. 'Lynch law's the beginnin' of anarchy.'

Hammond nodded, tight-lipped. He and his men had 'arrived' just after Fletcher, looking as shocked as everyone else. 'I'm with you there, Fletch.' Face innocent, he looked around at the other cowmen and nesters. 'At the same time, you look at young Ketchum and what they done to him for sparkin' one of their women.' He glared. 'Now I'd say that's a prime example of this anarchy Fletch was talkin' about! A kid of nineteen! Just feelin' his juices. Shot to hell.' He shook his head. 'I dunno. Reckon I can savvy why someone saw red and strung 'em up.'

'We dunno what happened to Ketchum. Sure, someone backshot him but we dunno who or why,' cautioned Fletcher.

Case Mannering spoke up. 'Yeah, I can savvy it all right, too. If it'd been my wife — if I had one — cheatin', I reckon I'd've gone after the feller once I knew who he was.'

'Well, I suppose it had to be Cattrell,' Fletcher allowed. He was a wizened man with ragged moustache and a cast in one eye. 'Never liked him. Mean bastard . . . '

'You're getting ahead of yourselves,' put in another rancher, Sewell. 'We just dunno what happened here. Who shot Johnny Richards an' left him for dead? *He* might be able to tell us somethin'.'

'If he lives,' growled one of the nesters. 'I don't like any of this.

'Specially the way *we're* bein' treated.'

There were growls of agreement from other nesters and Hammond held up one hand.

'Well, you can tell all your gripes to the deputy,' Hammond said, gesturing to a man coming over the rise on a running horse that had obviously been spurred and put to its limit. 'He's finally got here.'

The town deputy was at a loss what to do. He had nothing more than a few brawls and a regular bunch of drunks each Saturday night to contend with in his line of duty.

But, something like this! One look at his face and Hammond knew Deputy Frank Carmody was way out of his depth.

He was a man in his thirties, not keeping the best of health, and slow to make decisions. The deputy position had been specially created for him, when the sheriff's office was transferred to the county seat, a few miles to the north.

'Er, this is way beyond me. I ain't able to look into anythin' like this. Dunno enough law, or how to go about it.'

'Well, who the hell does?' demanded Fletcher.

Carmody looked at him soberly. 'A US marshal.'

Hammond stiffened and he and Case Mannering exchanged a startled glance. *They hadn't counted on that!*

'The hell we need a marshal for, Frank?' Linus Hammond demanded. 'This is local trouble! Call the sheriff.'

'A lynchin' is the same as murder — death without trial or due process. I know that much law. Soon as they told me I was needed out here, I sent a wire to the US marshal at Painted Rock. He'll arrive on tonight's stage.'

Hammond was tight-lipped. 'Talk about takin' a shotgun to kill a mouse!'

'No, Mr Hammond!' the deputy said sharply. 'I like my job and I take it seriously. But I know my limitations and what I'm s'posed to do an' what not. In this case, I need to get a marshal in here to take over. Meantime, I'd like statements from anyone who can tell

143

me anythin' at all about what might've happened here.'

He looked around hopefully but no one volunteered anything. Finally, Linus Hammond heaved a sigh.

'For Chris'sakes! Look, Frank, this is a terrible thing, right enough. But you used to be a cowhand before you started ailing. You know how it is between nesters and cattlemen. It's almost traditional that they're at each other's throats. And young Ray was a cowboy.'

'Traditional don't count when it comes to the letter of the law, Linus.'

'Don't look so goddamn smug!' Hammond glanced around at the gathering. 'I dunno if I can speak for anyone else, but personally, I have to admit I'm not too upset by this thing. Won't go so far as to say 'Good luck' to whoever done it, but — well, seems to me some future trouble has been nipped in the bud by these hangings. If certain folk are smart enough to take 'em as a warning.'

'Now you can't say that, Linus!' the

deputy said quickly, cutting off several of the nesters who wanted to protest. 'This is out-and-out flaunting of the law and it has to be set to rights! An' I'm still waiting for some kinda statement from someone.' Carmody looked around hopefully but all faces were blank, although one of the nesters said,

'Whyn't you try askin' *us* for statements?'

His friends murmured agreement and Carmody held up a hand. 'I reckon the marshal will take statements from everyone when he gets here, so for now, I'll just take down the names of all of you so he can follow through.'

Exasperated, the men shifted uncomfortably as the deputy took out a book and pencil.

'How about cuttin' down them Marchants?' snapped one of the nesters. 'If they was cowmen, I bet they'd be all laid out neat in a row, hands crossed on chests by this time, covered up so the crows couldn't get at 'em!'

There was a lot of grumbling after

that and Deputy Frank Carmody waited for it to fade some and then said, hesitantly, 'I guess it's all right to take 'em down.'

Hammond and Mannering exchanged sober glances: they weren't happy about a US marshal buying into this.

★ ★ ★

Marshal Dean Bowen came into the infirmary, boots clumping, and stopped beside the bed where Johnny Richards lay, his head heavily bandaged, face grey and drawn with pain. The doctor was a step behind the lawman and snapped, 'He's not really ready for an interrogation, Marshal.'

'Just a couple questions, Doc, that's all.' Dean Bowen was a tough-faced *hombre*, with eyes that tended to drill through you rather than just look. He was in his forties, experienced, and a by-the-book man, through and through.

The medic gently shook Richards by the shoulder and after a few moments the eyes flickered open. Recognition came swiftly and Johnny ran a tongue across his dry lips.

'How'm I — doin', Doc?'

'You're a lucky man. Your thick hair saved you, deflected the bullet just a fraction, so it more or less bounced off instead of penetrating your skull. This here is Marshal Dean Bowen, by the way. He wants — '

'Thanks, Doc, I'll take over.' Bowen waited while the medic moved away, frowning, looking a mite worriedly at Richards. 'Mr Richards, all I want to know is, can you tell me who lynched the Marchant family?'

Johnny looked at him and said quite clearly, 'Sure. It was Linus Hammond. I heard him give the order to his ramrod Case Mannering. He said 'Hang 'em all — the three men *and* the boy.''

Bowen was writing quickly in his notebook. 'He meant the Marchant family?'

Johnny Richards nodded, winced, murmured an affirmative. Bowen asked, 'You couldn't be mistaken . . . ?'

'No, I passed out right after, but I heard him give the order clear as I'm hearin' you speak now.'

The marshal surprised him by smiling. 'Mister, you dunno how glad I am to hear you say that!' At Richards' quizzical look, he lowered his voice and said, 'I've been after Linus Hammond for years — he and his brother Greg have been a thorn in our sides, for nigh on ten years now. Always managed to get away with whatever crime they pulled. If you're absolutely sure about this . . . ?'

'Absolutely,' Johnny assured him.

'Christ! I can hardly believe it! At last I've got Hammond just where I want the son of a bitch! I know damn well he an' his brother raided a Mormon wagon train and got away with a fortune in gold they were takin' to one of their settlements. It was my case but I got blocked every which way, trying to nail 'em. They were smart enough to use some of the gold to buy off a lot of folk who could've testified against them. I'll never nail 'em for that job now, but — ' He sobered suddenly. 'Listen, you will stand up in court and swear to this, won't you? I mean, you won't get cold feet?'

Frowning, brain throbbing, Richards shook his head slowly and cautiously. 'Why should I?'

Bowen sighed. 'Hammond's been known to . . . put pressure on witnesses. Sometimes they've met with an 'accident' just before the court hearing . . . '

Johnny stiffened. 'I'll swear to it in court. But if Hammond's that kind, you've got to guarantee the safety of my woman. We're to be married in June . . . '

'I'll do that.' With the pen poised over the paper, Johnny gave him Joanna's name and address.

'It better be done *right!* You gotta guarantee it.'

'She'll be guarded round the clock until the trial. So will you. Hell! I could *really* wrap this up if I had just one more witness — someone to back you up.' Johnny Richards' face sobered and Bowen frowned, leaned forward. 'You know someone else who can put Hammond right there at the lynching?' Bowen asked quickly. 'He claims he didn't arrive till later . . . the same as every other cowman there.'

After a hesitation, Johnny said, 'The Marchants were still alive when Diamond H cornered 'em. I tried to stop things and got shot for my trouble. They left me for dead, and strung up the Marchants. After they'd gone, a nester named Cattrell turned up. He gave me a little help, then disappeared before the deputy showed. But I think he — well, he'd had some trouble with Ray taking an interest in his wife. I gathered he'd . . . settled things with her, then came after Ketchum.'

'He'd intended to kill Ketchum himself?'

'Yeah, he was all set, but he was just too late, saw Case Mannering kill Ketchum, then Diamond H strung up the Marchants, and blamed the nesters

150

for killing Ray so as the other cowmen would sanction the lynching.'

Bowen suddenly smiled, but there was no warmth in it, just a movement of his lips. 'I need to talk with this Cattrell. Know where I can find him?'

Richards didn't answer at first, then when the 'Marshal asked again, more emphatically, he said, 'All I know is he's waiting to get his crack at Mannering for blaming him for backshooting Ray Ketchum.'

'Waiting — where?'

'Find Mannering and Cattrell won't be too far away.'

Richards looked past the marshal's shoulder and his pain-wracked face lit up as Joanna came hurrying into the infirmary. He flicked his gaze to the lawman who was checking his notes.

'Reckon you could do that someplace else, Marshal?'

'What? No, I may need to check something you said and — ' He jumped to his feet suddenly and swept off his hat, revealing sandy hair, a pink scalp showing through the strands. 'Ma'am, my apologies. I didn't see you. Take my chair. I was just going.' He looked at Richards who seemed brighter already now Jo was there. 'I'll come back later, Richards. Thanks for your help.'

They watched him go and then Joanna sat down on the edge of the bed, leaned down and kissed him lightly on the cheek.

'A little off-target,' he said, his hand seeking hers and finding it. Her grip was tight, seeking comfort.

'I'll find it after a while. Oh, John, I was so worried when they brought me word you'd been shot in the head.'

'Best place — solid bone. Can't hurt me.'

She smiled but there was a glisten to her eyes, too, as she leaned down and this time their lips brushed.

*   *   *

Marshal Dean Bowen wasn't a man to sit around and wait for things to happen — although he could do that, and often did because of circumstances. But when he had enough of a clue to get something done, he went at it without hesitation.

It took him five hours to find Cy Cattrell.

He figured the man would watch Diamond H and he had already learned from Deputy Carmody that Mannering was working at a line camp out near the northern border of the nesters' valley. It was a wise precaution to have someone in that area but Bowen wasn't able to determine if Mannering was alone or had a couple of sidekicks . . .

It was getting along towards sundown when he arrived in the foothills, having taken a couple of wrong turnings. He could smell woodsmoke, and a whiff of frying beefsteak. The lawman salivated but unsheathed his rifle as he came out of the trees and saw the cabin in the clearing.

There was only one horse in the corral and he smiled thinly. 'We'll just have us a man-to-man talk, I think, Mr Mannering,' he told himself quietly.

And then the peace of the approaching evening was shattered by gunfire.

Bowen hauled rein instantly, rammed his mount back into the shadow of the trees, levered a shell into the rifle's breech swiftly. While the startled horse settled, he stood in the stirrups, looking back towards the cabin where the shooting was growing in earnest now.

Glass shattered somewhere. A bullet snarled away in ricochet. Wood splintered. The door rattled as bullets peppered its planks.

Dismounted now, crouching, the marshal saw the smoke from the rifle upslope that was pouring lead into the lineshack. The man hammered away until his rifle was empty. Then, instead of reloading, he appeared, half-running, half-sliding down the slope. Bowen saw what the man intended to do and couldn't believe it: he was going to run straight at the door!

And Mannering was shooting from a

window only a couple of feet to the side.

The man staggered — he figured by now it must be Cy Cattrell from Johnny's description — but such was his passion Cattrell righted himself and kept coming, six-gun in fist now. He hit the door at full run. Luckily for him it tore loose from its leather hinges and the latch snapped off. He stumbled into the cabin's dimness and from where he crouched, the marshal could see the interior briefly lit by the leaping flashes of several gun shots.

By then the lawman was moving fast. He leapt over the hanging door, went in crouching and slammed back against the wall just inside.

There were two men sprawled on the floor, both bleeding, Mannering trying to reach his rifle which he had dropped. But there was blood trickling from his mouth and his eyes were glazing even as his fingers touched the weapon, and slid off as he slumped.

Cattrell was sitting up now against

the wall, holding his midriff, blood oozing between his fingers. He stared at the lawman, bared his teeth briefly, breath hissing in with ragged gasping sounds. 'It would be — you — they sent. Get his — dyin' confession that he — he killed young Ketchum, lawman, an' I'll swear 'twas Hammond give the order for the — lynchin'. I seen an' heard it all . . . '

Bowen nodded, thinking, *Might be yours'll be a dying confession, too, Cattrell, the way you look . . . but it'll carry a lot of weight in a court of law — a lot of weight. Just as long as it nails Linus Hammond . . .*

★   ★   ★

It did.

The judge accepted Cattrell's statement as a 'deathbed confession'. And Mannering, in terrible pain from a torn-up lung, admitted he had killed young Ketchum *and* that Hammond had given the order to lynch the Marchants.

These pieces of evidence, together with Richards' vital statement that he had actually *heard* Hammond give the order, sealed the rancher's doom: he was sentenced to hang at the Harwood Penitentiary fourteen days later . . .

Before then, Johnny Richards, now out of hospital and recovering from the head wound, received a visitor at Joanna's cousin's place. He was sitting, reading, under a tree in the yard when a big man sauntered up, his spurs jingling. Richards was startled: for a moment he thought it was Linus Hammond!

Then he saw that there was a strong resemblance although this man was older then Linus. He had a square jaw, rubbery lips which he half-pursed now and thumbed back his hat, revealing his round face. It was deeply tanned, but greyish in parts, and together with the way he walked, marked him down as a working cattleman. 'You Johnny Richards?'

Richards set down the book, wished

he was wearing his six-gun, although the other man made no hostile moves towards his own Colt.

'I'm Richards — what can I do for you?'

'Not a damn thing, 'less you wanna change your evidence you gave at the trial?'

'Not likely.'

'No, figured not. I'm Greg Hammond, Linus's brother.'

Johnny tensed now, aware of the cold steel in the man's voice and his confident, arrogant manner.

'Was your evidence that finally nailed Linus. The deathbed confession things were strong, but *you* were the live article and it was your evidence that swung the jury to bring in a guilty verdict — and the death penalty.'

He almost spat the last words.

'Your brother deserves it.'

'Shut up, you mealy-mouthed bastard! Deserve it or not, they're gonna hang him in five days — I can't stop it happenin'. But I can tell you this . . . '

Greg Hammond leaned forward, eyes like gun muzzles. 'I can tell you, that you're a dead man walkin'! Oh, I mightn't get at you right away, fact I reckon I'll feel better if I make you sweat for a spell, but you can bet I *will* get you.' He straightened and turned, started to walk away, then threw over his shoulder, 'An' that woman you figure on marryin' . . . '

Richards heaved up out of the chair but he still wasn't fully recovered and a wave of dizziness surged through him and he grabbed wildly at the chair arm. It overturned and he fell, trying to extricate himself from the chair legs.

Greg Hammond laughed — bitterly, mockingly.

'Glad the shock got to you. You'll have plenty of time to think about it, and worry about it. Just make sure you believe that no matter what, it will happen. First the bitch, then you. Get better soon, Richards. I want you up an' around, worryin' your guts out, you son of a bitch! Just one more thing: I

159

was never here. You can complain to your marshal and whoever you like, but you'll find I can prove I wasn't within ten miles of this dump at any time. Hey! Mebbe you ain't gettin' better as fast as you thought. You're breaking out in a sweat — I hope it's a good cold one! You'll have a lot more comin'!'

He spat and turned away, whistling, confident, like a man who considers he's just done a good day's work. But his face was a sickly colour and his left hand crept up under his shirt and massaged his chest, which felt as if he had a horse standing on it . . .

Mebbe that sawbones in Tucson was right. Maybe he ought to go see a specialist about the state of his heart. Maybe.

But he sure would like to live long enough to see this Richards suffer all he had planned for him.

He'd do anything for that . . .

9

The Long Arm

The town of Harwood was the county seat and the businessmen got together and decided they could use the hanging day for profit.

They went to work on the authorities and the men involved and finally got the 'OK' for a hanging day party.

The handbills and notices went out well beyond the confines of the county — everyone was invited to a 'picnic day that will forever stay in the memory! The death of a mass murderer who thought his wealth and power would save him from any crime he cared to commit.'

The crowd poured in, by train, stagecoach, ranch wagons, buggies, surreys, horseback and even on foot.

Joanna and Johnny had no desire to

see the execution but Richards felt he would be a lot happier when Linus Hammond was dead.

But only then, according to Greg Hammond, would his real nightmare begin . . .

And it began soon after Linus Hammond kicked his last feeble dying gesture at the end of the hangman's rope.

Some said later, getting a mite fanciful, that Linus had reached out from beyond the grave to square with Johnny Richards for giving the evidence that finally decided his fate . . .

Greg Hammond had obviously been waiting for him, Richards thought afterwards: he was grooming the sorrel in the stables behind the house when Hammond suddenly appeared, a couple of hard-faced cowboys either side.

Johnny tensed, dropped the curry comb, freeing his gunhand. Greg Hammond held up a hand.

'Relax — for now. Enjoy what you can, while you can, Richards. Just got a few words to say.' He was breathing hard and one hand involuntarily rubbed at the left side of his chest as his narrowed eyes bored into Johnny. 'You got Linus killed, an' you're gonna die because of it.' He flicked his gaze towards the house. 'And your woman — just wanted to make sure you don't forget. You won't know when it's comin' or, even if anythin' starts, if it's gonna finish. Might just be a reminder to you that I got a long memory. Nice hoss you got there. It's yours, so mebbe you better keep a good close eye on it, too.'

'You're repeatin' yourself, Hammond. Go away and die somewhere. I'll help you do it any time.'

Greg forced a smile. 'I just bet you would — but you'll never get the chance. *Adios*, you son of a bitch. Just keep lookin' over your shoulder . . . '

They backed away and Richards watched them go, frowning. Not scared for himself, but what about Jo when he was away working . . . ? *Damnit! Greg's threats were already getting to him!*

Greg Hammond didn't let the grass grow under him: he reached one of Bowen's guards, a man named Hatton.

'I hear the marshals' pay ain't very big,' Greg Hammond said to the man when he managed to corner him in the bar of the saloon he owned. *He wasn't feeling so chipper, the hanging too fresh in his mind. Mebbe if he could pull off this spur-of-the-moment idea, he'd feel better, despite what the damn doctors kept saying about his failing heart . . .*

Hatton used some of his beer to wash down the whiskey Hammond had bought. 'It ain't much,' he admitted, a narrow-faced man, medium size. 'I could use a better job. Feller I know in 'Frisco runs a boat south — special cargo.' He paused and winked. 'Needs men to guard it. My kinda job . . . if I can get there.'

'Sounds interestin'. How much would it cost to get you there?'

Hatton turned his head slowly, sipped some more beer. 'I'd say a fair lot, countin' livin' expenses.'

'Yeah, that figures. Mebbe you just need a raise.'

'Well, I guess I wouldn't get paid for doin' nothin'.'

'Maybe not 'nothin' '. But might be if you *didn't* do somethin' it could earn you a few bucks.'

Hatton seemed to freeze with his beer glass halfway to his mouth. 'Now that could cost a lot . . .

'Name a figure and let's dicker.'

★   ★   ★

Hatton was a fool. Greedy, maybe a little drunk on the whiskey and beer Hammond had paid for. Just a damn fool.

And he blew it . . .

He heard the shooting up in the brush behind Joanna's cousin's place, a smallholding near the edge of town. The shots were spaced fairly regularly and he reckoned Richards was practising now he was recovering from his head wound. Greg Hammond was paying him a thousand dollars — half down now, the rest when he had done the chore — *plus* a fast horse. *If Richards was busy, now might be a good time . . .*

Eager to get all that money in his pocket, Hatton went boldly up to the front door of the house and rapped the knocker. He knew Temple, Joanna's cousin, was at the cattle agency looking over a herd of milk cows . . . and with Richards up in the brush, the woman would be alone in the house.

Joanna opened the door, wearing a floury apron over her house dress. She knew Hatton by sight, him being one of the 'bodyguards' Bowen had arranged for. She didn't like the man but had put her dislike aside because he was supposed to be guarding her and Johnny.

He touched a hand to his hatbrim. 'Sorry to disturb you, Miss Craig. Wonder if I could step in for a minute . . . ? Mr Harris, the head guard, sent me down. Somethin's come up about your man, Johnny Richards, and Harris needs for me to check it out with you.'

Jo frowned. 'What — 'something'?'

Hatton looked around, trying to appear anxious. He lowered his voice. 'Well, it's kinda — private, ma'am. He was starting to edge his way in past the door and Joanna made up her mind: she didn't trust this man! So she started to slam the door, but he had his shoulder against the panel and shoved back hard. Joanna cried out, staggering. The apron was caught by the door edge and half of it flapped outside, the now-taut tapes holding her as she made to run.

She jerked back, snapping the tape, and was still righting herself when he reached for her, eyes slitted and burning lasciviously now. He ripped at her bodice.

She screamed and his smile of anticipation stiffened. He swung an open hand and caught her across the

167

face. The blow knocked her sprawling, stunned. Hatton bared his teeth as he stooped to rip her dress away . . .

The door was kicked in behind him, just scraping his buttocks, sending him staggering. He whirled, off balance, snatching at his six-gun. His eyes flew wide as he saw Richards standing there, grim-faced. He had been returning to the house when he had seen the apron caught in the door, then heard Joanna scream.

'Go for it, you snake!' Johnny gritted and Hatton lifted his gun in a flash, very fast.

But Richards' Colt *bammed!* twice, the first bullet knocking Hatton down the passage. He slammed against the wall, brought his gun up, just in time for the second slug to punch him in the chest and fling him through the doorway of the parlour.

Richards had his gun bolstered before Hatton crumpled, helping the shocked Joanna to her feet. She came in against him, grasping desperately, and he slid his free hand around her waist, pulling her in tightly. He folded her in his arms as the sobs shook her . . .

* * *

'It had to be Hammond behind this,' Marshal Dean Bowen said as he waited out on Doc MacAllister's porch with Richards. 'Greg must've got to Hatton, who may be a good man with a gun, but he's always been hungry for money: he had almost five hundred bucks on him. I'd say Greg told him to assault Joanna, just as a way of thumbing his nose at you, lettin' you know he can carry out his threats.'

'Time I had a word with that sonuver.'

Bowen shook his head. 'No point, you'll never prove Hammond even knew Hatton, let alone fixed a deal with him.'

'Jo's had a scare, a damn big one, but Doc says she'll be OK. Be obliged if you'd stay with her till I get back.'

'Wait! Where the hell you think you're goin'?'

By then Richards was leaving by the side door.

He went to the Brighteyes saloon and didn't stop after he straight-armed the batwings open. His hard gaze slid around the smoky bar swiftly, saw Greg Hammond with three other men at a rear table, drinks before them, some cards scattered across the green baize.

They saw him, too and tensed as he came striding straight up, startling them: it looked as if he was going to climb right over the table. Two of the men leapt to their feet and Richard's gun came up in a single sweeping arc, clouting their heads, dropping them cold. The other man had his gun half-drawn but froze when Johnny's bleak gaze touched him. Greg Hammond couldn't get out of his chair because Richards was standing over him so close. He suddenly grabbed the startled rancher by the shirtfront, yanked him upright.

Then Richards' gun barrel whipped back and forth across the rancher's head and face, the foresight laying open the flesh. Hammond sagged, limp as a rag doll, barely conscious, as Johnny swung him around into the third man, who, belatedly, started to bring his gun up all the way.

Hammond's body knocked him sprawling across the two on the floor. Richards held his grip on Hammond's shirt, shook him, the man's bloody head rocking limply. But his eyes had a little focus in them.

Enough for him to savvy what Richards had to say . . .

'You warned me, you bastard! This is my warning to you. Any of your men come even *within sight* of Joanna and I'll kill them! Quit while you're ahead, Hammond. You figure you're tough and run things your way, well, I do things my way, too. You ain't seen me properly riled yet. This is nothin' — just a warning. If you're smart you'll take heed.'

He flung the mauled rancher down on top of his groaning men, turned and strode out past the stunned drinkers.

No one tried to stop him.

* * *

'Judas priest!' exploded Dean Bowen. 'You *are* loco! Tacklin' someone like Greg Hammond that way . . . in his own saloon!' He was breathing hard, made himself settle down. 'Not that I, personally, disapprove, but Hammond's got a lot of pull and the chief marshal will have pressure put on him once Greg lodges an official complaint. He's a big-time rancher and it counts, I'm sorry to say.'

'Mebbe not,' Johnny broke in. 'He wants to get me personally. He won't want any US marshal stepping in and taking me to task.'

Bowen looked dubious, ran a hand across his stubbled jaw. 'We-ell, that's possible, but Greg won't take it lying down. He could blow up and turn loose

172

his bunch of killers on you and Joanna.'

'That's OK by me.'

'Don't be a fool man! If Greg decided to cut loose even the marshals couldn't stop him in time. You and Joanna would be dead! And, I'd guess, she would be first to go — so you could see it happen.'

Richards' jaw muscles knotted at the thought. He released a long breath and nodded. 'Yeah, you're likely right. Long time since I've blown up like that. So, what do we do?'

Bowen looked at him steadily, seemed hesitant.

'Well — what?' demanded Johnny, noticing the lawman's apparent reluctance.

'Actually, we had a . . . situation like this once before. People we needed to give vital evidence against an outlaw syndicate we wanted out of business at all costs. What we did was move our witnesses to a safe place, gave 'em new names and backgrounds and kept them hidden until it was time for the case to be heard by a judge. Worked, too. Nailed the outlaws good.'

Johnny could see the man was remembering the incident and cut in impatiently: 'What happened to the witnesses afterwards?'

Again that slight hesitation before Bowen spoke. 'We made a new life for them. Set 'em up with new identities, sent 'em a long way off, different jobs to what they'd ever done before and so on. Feller grew a moustache, later, a beard. Woman dyed her hair, did it in a different style. They're doin' just fine now. No one knows who they really are . . . except the chief marshal and his head deputy.'

Johnny frowned. 'The idea sounds all right.'

'But . . . ?'

'I dunno. I've already given my evidence.'

'And now your life's in danger — so is Joanna's, which is likely more important the way you think. We appreciate you standing up and nailing Linus for us, Johnny. You could figure this as our way of showing our gratitude.'

'A complete disruption of our lives?'

'You see it that way? I'm surprised. You got brains, you must see that someone like Greg won't ever give up. The service couldn't guarantee a hatful of bodyguards to watch over you for the rest of your lives.'

'I wouldn't want that, anyway. Look, Dean, I figure I could come to terms eventually with what you're suggesting, but, well, I dunno about Jo. She's always been a stickler for people and their families — who they are, their background, their ancestors. Somethin' she's very particular about, possibly because her father was a 'foundling' as she calls it, bein' polite. He never knew his parents, had no family at all he knew about. Now, you're askin' her to get married under a name that's not even hers.'

Bowen was silent for a few minutes. 'All right. Suppose I arrange a name-change for you both? *Legally*. There are ways and we've done it at least once before that I know of, likely more. You can have a totally legal marriage and live by totally legal names. And Greg Hammond will never find you.'

'That's the part I care about, otherwise I wouldn't even listen to you. Even now, I figure I could put an end to the threat by goin' after Greg.'

Bowen shook his head. 'The chief's a hard man, Johnny, and his is a political appointment. He could never agree to you going after Greg Hammond, even if he felt you could take care of it — and if you went, anyway, he'd have no hesitation in putting you on the 'Wanted' list.'

'Hell almighty!' Richards wanted to swear a string of oaths but forced himself to restrain. 'How the hell does he sleep nights?'

'You'd have to ask him. Look, my way is the only way you'll stay beyond Greg's long arm, Johnny. Think about it, but don't take too damn long! You've hit him where he lives and he won't rest till he squares it away. I reckon it'll even take precedence over avenging Linus. You've got yourself a whole slew of trouble, feller. And I'm not sure I can keep you and Jo alive — unless you do what I say.'

10

Next Move

Sheriff Vince Starrett eased his buttocks on his desk chair, elbows on the seat arms, and steepled his fingers. His face was expressionless, but there was an intensity about his eyes as he regarded the man he knew as Martin Sands.

'I suppose that's as close as you need to come to the present. I mean, we can take it as read, that Flagstaff was where Marshal Bowen 'settled' you and after young Jason Craig's unfortunate death, with the passage of a decent interval, you and Miss Joanna decided to tie the knot.'

Martin Sands nodded slowly. 'I can tell you'd rather have more details, Vince, but let me just say this: Flagstaff wasn't the first place Bowen moved us to.'

Starrett eased his upper body forward. 'Oh?'

'No. It was a stupid mistake, and the marshals made it. We moved on to a town called Ponystroke. You likely don't know it . . . '

'Population about three hundred, including the pariah dogs. On the banks of a stretch of the Mississippi locals call the 'Barley Sugar' because of all the twists and turns.'

Sands arched his eyebrows. 'That's it. You know what was wrong with the move?'

'Sure — not enough permanent population. New arrivals couldn't just disappear into the crowds — because there weren't any to speak of. Was that it?'

'Yeah. We were on show right from the start. Bowen was supposed to set us up with a quarter-section and that meant registering with the land agency. Then some fool forwarded our baggage with our new names on the tags. But he'd started to write 'Richards' on one and just scratched it through with a pen stroke before putting 'Sands' beside it. Two gunmen turned up within a week — we left a couple days later.'

'And the gunmen . . . ?'

'They're still there — in the Ponystroke cemetery.'

Starrett stared a little, then moved his head side to side. 'You kept well within your character, I see.'

Sands ignored that.

'Then we came here. Looked good for a time, then I was stupid: entered that rodeo and rode Hellboy right into the newspapers with my name and picture.' He shook his head irritably. 'Just through stupid desperation to get enough money to make a move.'

The lawman tapped his manicured fingers against his desk again, narrowed his eyes. 'But you sound kind of annoyed at the prospect of another move.'

'I think 'pissed' fits better. Two moves already. Just get really settled and — all I can say is Bowen better make the next one permanent.'

The lawman frowned. 'What can you do? You have to make the moves now, or you're dead!'

Martin Sands stood wearily. 'That's what everyone keeps telling us.' He glanced at the old loud-ticking wall clock. 'I need to see Jo and talk this over with her, Vince.'

Starrett stood, hesitated and reached across the desk with his right hand outstretched, 'Good luck, Martin — or whatever name you settle on. If you think I can be of any help don't hesitate to wire me.' He smiled wryly. 'Address it to 'Mr Deacon' and I'll know.'

'Obliged, Vince. I'll remember that.'

They gripped firmly and as Sands turned towards the street door, moving as fast as he was able, the sheriff said quietly, 'The marshals don't always find a good safe place for folk they're supposed to protect.'

Sands paused, frowning as he turned. 'What're you saying, Vince?'

'Look, sit down for a few minutes. No, I won't detain you from seeing

Joanna for long, but — well, this could change your life — or make sure you have one . . . '

Frowning more deeply, Sands dropped into his chair again. The sheriff stared back steadily.

'I know of Dean Bowen. He's good at his job but I also know of a man he helped, call him Jeff, who had several dodgers out on him — he was a gunfighter, lived on the contents of strongboxes, mostly: other folks' strong-boxes.'

'An outlaw, in other words.'

'Uh-huh — a true 'badman'. He didn't kill unless forced into it but he chalked up an enviable score, just the same.'

'You're talkin' about Snake Jefferson, aren't you? They said no rattler could strike faster than he could get his gun out.'

Starrett made a 'leave-it' gesture. 'He got . . . involved with a gang who was run by a prominent politician in a certain State — Territory, it was then.

No one could ever prove the politician's involvement but with his access to times of shipping payrolls and money for civilian public works he set up the robberies and grew rich — untouchable.'

Sands looked up at the wall clock. 'Move it along, Vince.'

'All right — Jeff killed some of the gang in an argument over divvying-up, and the politician happened to be there and was wounded. As was Jeff. A posse found them and — to cut things short — in jail, the marshals put it to Jeff: give evidence that the politician was at the robbery scene, directing it, and all charges would be dropped. He would be given a new identity and set up in a law-abiding life.'

'And . . . ?'

Half-smiling Starrett lifted a hand. 'It went well, but people can be bought and some are just plain dumb. Jeff had to make three moves before he decided he could disappear without the help of the marshals.'

Martin Sands tensed. 'He went it

alone?' When Vince nodded, he added, 'Well, I heard this Snake Jefferson just disappeared, but like everyone else I figured someone from his past had killed him.'

'They — I believe they tried, but he gave them the slip.' He paused. 'Sometimes it's better to hide in a prominent place, than look for a dark corner, Martin.'

'What's that mean?'

'Well, for instance, who would figure a wild outlaw like Jeff, say, might become a lawman? That'd be the last place anyone would look for him. Or, he could, maybe become a storekeeper, livery man, even a preacher — or be affiliated some way with a church — if he felt he wanted to atone for some of his . . . misdeeds.' He added quickly as Sands gave him a sharp look. 'I'm theorizing, just to illustrate that you could arrange your own disappearance without a third party being involved — and avoid that much of the risk of being exposed.'

Sands stared hard. 'Vince, you wouldn't be talking about — '

'It's just an example that might help you and Joanna,' Starrett cut in, stood and stretched out his hand again. 'I've been told this story about Jeff and the fact is — to all intents and purposes he *has disappeared*. Give the matter some thought, Martin. And best of luck.'

This time, the handgrip was firmer, the eye-to-eye contact steadier.

'You, too,' Sands murmured, half-smiling.

★   ★   ★

When Dean Bowen came, he was angry.

'Of all the damned fool things to do!' he snapped, ignoring Sands' out-stretched hand. The marshal was too angry; he dropped a valise on a chair and began to pace back and forth in the small cabin.

'What in *hell* were you thinking of! Entering a rodeo with guaranteed national publicity!'

Sands sat down and started to build a cigarette. 'There's nothing new you can tell me about how stupid I was, Dean. Jo's anxious to get a proper home, a place we can really settle — she thinks she might be pregnant, too, and wants somewhere decent, and safe, for a kid to grow up. I got kinda desperate for money.'

'I can savvy that. But. Jo's an intelligent woman. She can surely hold off long enough to make absolutely sure you're safe.'

Sands lit up, squinted through the smoke. 'You didn't give us enough details, Dean. You didn't say there might be a whole series of moves involved.'

'Damnit, surely you realized that!'

'Well, maybe I did, but not sure Jo saw it that way. But when a woman's pregnant, well, she'd been hinting we should find a place and get it established before the baby was due. Not nagging, but every chance she got she mentioned it or twisted the subject around so it could be brought into the conversation.'

'They can do that,' Bowen said tersely, and Sands realized he had stirred some unwanted memories in the lawman.

'OK. Well, I used to be a pretty good broncbuster and I saw the chance to make some money that would set us up.' He spread his hands, shrugged. 'It was stupid.'

'We've already established that. Forget it. The damage has been done and you've made one helluva lot of work for me.'

Sands' jaw hardened. 'Where's that 'gratitude' you mentioned once?'

Bowen glared, suddenly stopped walking about and then dropped into a chair at the other side of the deal table where Sands sat. They looked at each other and then the lawman sighed.

'OK, I stopped by the doctor's on the way in and he tells me Jo will recover. No permanent damage. So you want somewhere you'll be able to set down roots, have it ready by the time the baby's born?' He shook his head slowly. 'You sure can gimme a hard time of it without even tryin'.'

Sands leaned forward. 'The kinda thing Jo pointed out: the names that aren't our own. Trying to remember if this time she's Mary Smith, or was that last time? No, then it was Lucy Whoever. You know what I mean?'

'I do — I lost a very good friend once who forgot who she was supposed to be, and it got her killed.'

Sands said nothing, let the silence drag on until the marshal broke it.

'Look, can we be practical about this, John? Damnit, *Martin!* Forget this area, in fact forget the whole damn Territory. Pick somewhere else. I'll help you or I'll make the decision if you don't want to risk Jo having some reservations.' Bowen glared. 'We'd better bring her into this, make it a three-way deal — majority decides.'

Sands hesitated. 'Rather it was unanimous.'

'Well, go see the doctor about when she can come home permanently and we'll get things moving. There's a hell of a lot involved, not the least being how to get you away from here without anyone knowing. It means dead-of-night stuff, so Jo has to be fit enough for some hard riding.'

'Not too damn hard! She's pregnant *and* still recovering from the wound.'

Bowen heaved another sigh. 'Go see the doctor — that'll be a start.' He indicated the leather valise he had tossed on to a chair when he had first arrived 'I'll get the papers ready and we can start planning when she gets here.'

Sands paused at the door, looked back at Bowen already taking papers from the valise.

'This had better be a damn good move, Dean.'

Bowen merely stared back and waited until Sands had left before starting to sort his papers.

★ ★ ★

189

They settled on Carson City, Nevada. It had been chosen, and officially recognized as the Capital of Nevada in 1864, a few years after the big gold and silver strikes at Comstock put it on the map.

At the foot of the Sierra Nevadas, which drove the clouds high and left the land beneath verdant but free of floods, the equable climate and the gold and silver ore discoveries gave birth to a huge transportation industry and Carson City became a thriving commercial centre.

As well, there was fine timber within a frog's leap of the town's boundaries and huge, miles-long shallow flumes were built to carry the felled logs down from the steep Spooner Summit to sawmills whose appetite never seemed to be appeased. Here the timber was trimmed and dressed into props for the mines, ties for the railroad, planed and shaped for clapboard houses and commercial buildings.

There was work for anyone who had the muscles and the wherewithal to earn top money almost anywhere in Ormsby County — the town Fathers had named the county after a long-dead hero of the Battle of Pyramid Lake.

The population was well into the five figures and fluctuated constantly — big money drew in the itinerant workers for the big pay available in the booming town.

Martin Sands — *Ooops!* — now Bob Dawson, with his wife Teresa or Tess, came to a double-storied house on the edge of town where, from the upstairs balcony, they could just catch a glimpe of the lake. They could also see the Warm Springs Hotel which one of the rich Founding Fathers had built a mile east of town. But, for some reason, instead of filling the rooms with a constant stream of paying guests, he hired it out for functions and, after a while, the government even leased it for a state prison.

The building itself was stylish enough, certainly no eyesore, but Joanna — now Tess Dawson — did not feel comfortable living within sight of a prison. 'Husband'

Bob savvied her concern, though it wasn't likely anyone could escape. He had plenty of reservations about this Carson City himself. The marshals' department had made it sound attractive, but he couldn't help remember Vince Starrett's story about the mysterious 'Jeff' . . . who went it alone.

His job in the valley sawmill paid well but had its drawbacks: not the least being the constant noise, the ring and grating of the giant spinning saw blades which near drove him cazy. His head was buzzing with the noise, punishing his ears for hours after he had quit work and walked to his new home. Some of the trees were scorched and actually smoking from hitting against the sides of the flume on their long, long journey down from the sierras, making for more hazards on the job: manhandling such logs was dangerous. He had already seen one man badly burned when his hand penetrated what seemed like a solid section of smouldering log: but it was aglow beneath a thin cladding of bark, red hot coals burning out from the inside cooked the man's hand.

Tess had got to hear about it — the victim was the husband of someone she'd met when shopping for the house food. She had immediately begun worrying about Bob and urged him to ask for a transfer.

'I haven't been working there but a few weeks, Jo — Tess! and — '

He paused, seeing her angry face. 'Oh, haven't you learned yet to use our new names! If you're not careful, you'll make the same mistake within the hearing of someone who might wonder about it — or even worse.'

He felt himself bristle but forced down the angry retort. His mouth tightened beneath the frontier moustache that was beginning to grow again — his concession to some form of disguise. 'I'm sorry, hon. It's just that this damn head-ringing is driving me nuts.'

'Try tying a kerchief over your ears,' she said, smiling. 'You'll look like one of the old English sailors fighting a sea battle. They used to tie a scarf over their ears to deaden the sounds of the cannons firing.'

He stared, half-smiled to himself. 'Bet I'd make a pretty picture.'

She laughed briefly, sobered when she saw his face.

'Tess, truth is, I hate the damn job! It wouldn't matter if they gave me somewhere quieter, It's not the actual work, I don't mind that part.' He paused. 'What's really wrong is — it's *inside*, and I'm an outdoor man, always have been. I'd be happier fellin' the damn trees in the sierras, even.'

She reached out and placed a finger across his lips, her eyes soft. 'Hush . . . Bob. *See?* I had to pause a moment and think about your name, too . . . '

He took her hand and kissed it, held it as he spoke, quite soberly.

'It's obvious, isn't it? Neither of us are happy here, nor likely to be. We're in the wrong place.'

'It did sound quite good at first . . . '

'Yeah. But — well, I know we have to make a lot of adjustments, but — hell! Why can't we do it somewhere we like?'

She looked up into his worried face, seeing the faint dusting of sawdust across his chin and one cheek. She brushed it absently as she said, 'Marshal Bowen isn't going to be pleased if we ask for another move so soon.'

'He'll probably be mad enough to save Greg Hammond the trouble and shoot us both!'

'It's not really funny, Johnny — Oh, to blazes with it! I slipped up on your name again.'

He was going to mention Vince Starrett's suggestion about making the move themselves, but decided to wait until they saw what Dean Bowen had to say.

11

One More Time

But Bowen sent a subordinate to handle the change.

'Man, Ol' Dean's ready to spit fire over this,' the marshal told an unrepentant Jo and Johnny Richards. (Though officially, they were Mr and Mrs Martin Sands, they thought of themselves by their real names.)

He was a fairly brash sort, and clearly believed that his marshal's standing allowed him to walk the earth with a special gait that wise folk would notice and clear the way for. He was called Hart Rebo, late twenties, long fair hair which he obviously liked to keep neat and visible. He removed his hat at every possible moment, using his free hand to pass lightly over the long side hair, swept back past his ears. The way he looked at women told Johnny Richards here was a man who, as his old man used to say of dandified card players, 'Likely kisses himself goodnight.'

Now, in the parlour, with Jo and Johnny sitting on the edge of their rented sofa, Rebo winked one of his pale blue eyes, flashed his white teeth. 'Dean hates paperwork, lets it get him down. Me, I don't worry about it. I get papers I gotta sign, I sign 'em and forget 'em.'

'I hope you read them first,' Jo said.

'Lady, I got my own life to lead. It don't rate me spending more time than I need showing the chief marshal how good I am at my job. He'll make up his own mind, anyways, and if he don't like it — ' He shrugged. 'O-K! Let's see if we can get you folks set-up someplace you might like.'

He took some folded papers from the pocket of his jacket which he had hung over the back of a chair as soon as he entered. Johnny figured it was so he could show off his biceps, for he had his shirt sleeves rolled up tight to his armpits. If Jo was impressed — and it had to be aimed at her — she didn't show it.

Rebo unfolded the papers and smoothed them out. 'All righty, what we got here . . . Texas? Nah, you ain't got anythin' like a Lone Star drawl and that'd get people wonderin' right off. Kansas? Sunshine State, sunflowers and sonsabitches.' He flicked his gaze at Jo but her face remained unchanged. 'Colorado — now, there's a go-ahead place. Gold turnin' up here and there, big camps, lots of strangers. You wouldn't be noticed there.'

'We don't want to live on any goldfields, Marshal,' Joanna told him flatly.

Rebo arched his eyebrows, glanced at Johnny, and ran a pencil through Colorado. 'Ask me, and I'd say it was pretty good there, but how about you tell me where you'd like to go and I'll tell you if it can be done.'

Johnny and Joanna exchanged a

glance and Richards said, 'Bowen promised us some land we could work and develop — it's what we've had in mind. Build somewhere for the baby when it comes and — '

Hart Rebo looked boldly at Jo and made her flush when he said, 'Baby, huh? You can't tell you're carryin' just by lookin' at you. You holdin' a damn good shape there, lady — *Hey! What the hell're you doin'?*'

Richards had grabbed the man by his sleeked-back hair, jerked his head back and towered over him, one fist cocked. 'I got some cattle dip I been savin', mister, and I'll be happy to wash your mouth out with it. Now you apologize to my wife or I'll bust you so good I might even have trouble finding where your mouth is.'

'Goddamnit! Get your hands off me!'

Rebo came out of the chair fast, raging, swinging at Johnny, who let the blow skid across one shoulder. He punched the man hard in the face, a driving straight-arm punch, and Rebo gave a womanish scream as he clawed at his blood-spurting nose. He crashed over the chair and landed in a crouching position. He tore off his colourful neckerchief and wadded it over his nose, hands shaking. His eyes were murderous as he looked at Johnny over the folds of cloth. 'My face! You bust my goddamn nose!'

'And I'll loosen every tooth in your stupid head — Now, cut the cussing and make that apology.'

'The hell with you!' Rebo went for his gun and his breath came out in a long, dwindling hiss as he stared into the muzzle of Richards' Colt. 'Kerrrrrist! How did you . . . ?'

The gun barrel jerked towards the tensed Joanna. 'My wife's over there. You got somethin' to say to her?'

Hart Rebo glared and then swallowed audibly as he turned, lowered the blood-soaked kerchief and mumbled, 'I — I'm sorry, ma'am. I meant no — disrepect.'

'Very nicely put, Marshal. Now pick

up your hat and get out.'

'I'm not finished here.'

'You are.'

Rebo shook his head as he moved slowly towards the door, watching Johnny closely. 'No — I ain't finished with *you*, I meant.'

'Well, you give that some more thought and we'll see, OK?'

When he came back from pushing Rebo out the front door, Joanna was standing at the table holding the marshal's folded papers. She glanced at her husband, a little pale.

'There are a lot of choices here, mostly in Bowen's handwriting.'

'Well, let's look at them and mebbe we can pick one . . . Or find one on our own.'

She sharpened her gaze. 'What — does that mean, exactly?'

'What did it sound like?'

She hesitated. 'For a moment, I thought you meant *we'd* pick a place and just — go. Without notifying Dean Bowen or anyone else.'

He slid an arm about her waist, looking down into her questioning face. 'Why not? We don't have to go anywhere that's on that list. We can choose a place of our own. I know at least one man who's done it — successfully.'

'But that — that would mean we have no protection!'

He slapped a hand against his gun butt. 'Who says?'

She stepped away from him, white teeth tugging at a corner of her lip. 'D'you know what you're proposing?'

'Damn right I do. Look, Bowen's all right, I'd say. But Hart Rebo's a flash idiot who spends most of his time in front of a mirror combing his hair. You think he wouldn't brag to some gal he's wantin' to impress, by telling her how he was given the job of setting up a couple of fools who, because they tried to do the right thing, have now got to hide from men like Greg Hammond?' He snapped his fingers. 'Rebo wouldn't even hesitate if it'd get him closer to some floosie's bed.'

She thought about it and agreed, but still wasn't certain they should make their run — as Johnny called it — on their own.

'Look, we're both having trouble remembering what names we're supposed to be using, Jo. Personally, I damn well hate callin' you anythin' else but Jo or Joanna.'

She nodded slowly. 'It is something of a darn nuisance,' she admitted.

'We can leave tonight — just walk away. Leave our clothes and luggage, make a new start from scratch. We can slip away from a town like this without anyone noticing. We've got a little money, thanks to that lousy job I was doing at the sawmill: it'll be enough to give us a fresh start. All we have to do is pick a place.'

He pushed an unfolded map across the table. Rebo had kept it beside his papers and there were a couple of splashes of blood from when his nose had been broken.

She just stared at him for a long minute.

Then she took a deep breath, closed her eyes, waved her hand about and stabbed downwards. 'There!'

Her finger, smearing a dot of Rebo's blood that hadn't quite dried, landed on a place called Colorado Springs, El Paso County, Colorado.

*   *   *

The town was a surprise to them both. It was more a city than a town. They hadn't realized that this was a *planned* community, started by one General William Palmer who had tired and disapproved of the nearby cowboy town of Colorado City — a misnomer, but perhaps someone had great expectations for the town when it was first established.

They didn't come to pass. Right from the start it was a wild-west town in the best — or worst — sense of the word. Shootings in the streets and saloons, liquor flowing day and night, girlie parlours by the street-load. Palmer was a mite stuffy *and* he was wealthy. So he purchased land near Pikes Peak at the southern end of the Rockies, and set about building his new town, and what was to become known internationally as 'The Antlers' Resort.

It catered for folk with fully-lined, bulging wallets, from both the United States and overseas: at the time Jo and Johnny arrived the place was even tagged 'Little London' because so many Britishers came for the high, dry climate — the town was six thousand feet up in the Rockies and enjoyed a wonderful climate, sheltered by the mountains.

Stuffy as ever, General Palmer determined his projected city would be alcohol free — though later 'druggists' proliferated and advertised (legally) 'Imported whisky, stout, ale and beer — for medicinal purposes only.'

Not too many purchasers took any notice of that last word. But anyone with a real mind for what passed as a 'good ol' high-time' could ride the few miles to Colorado City and hit the wide-open saloons and cathouses.

Despite the juggling of drawbacks and advantages, one thing decided the Richards on choosing to live in 'The Springs' as it was called. General Palmer had seen to it that there were excellent medical facilities and hospitals, perhaps the best in the country, next to Denver, which was said to have the top medical care in the West — and it was only sixty miles to the north, anyway.

'I hope it'll be a straight, uncomplicated birth,' Joanna confessed. 'But, well, I can't help but want to take precautions — just in case, Johnny.'

He took her in his arms. 'You're a good wife, Jo, and I'll be with you all the way. This is a pretty good place for you here, maybe a mite close to the rail yards, but it's near to stores and places you might need to go to.' She nodded and he took a deep breath. 'Fine! Now,

I think — ' He paused and she looked up at him, body tensing as she sensed something she wasn't going to like. 'I think I better ride out to Cripple Creek where they've just made that new gold strike.'

'Oh, no, John! You said you wouldn't go to the gold fields!'

'Hon, it took a lot more of our money than I figured to get here and, now we're here, well it's pretty expensive just to live, day-to-day, but it's a good place for us. We're gonna need the money. I was talking to a couple of fellers down at the general store. They've been there and hit a rich vein — it's happening all over. They say it's gonna be one of the biggest gold strikes in the world . . . '

'Oh, they say that about every field that might go well for a few weeks or months and then — '

'I went to see an assayer, hon. I knew him a few years ago, recognized his name on his office sign. This is the real thing, a genuine *big* strike and there's

207

gonna be a rush. If we want to get our share, I've got to get out there fast.' She started to speak but he went on, overriding her words. 'There'll be enough cash left over after I get you settled in for me to outfit myself. If I don't hit good colour in a couple of weeks, I'll know it's just another ordinary strike, blown up out of all proportion, and I'll come back.'

It still wasn't easy to convince her and, he had to be honest: he didn't really want to go stake a claim and live on the goldfields again. He'd done it twice before in his life and it was *rough* — not to mention downright danger-ous.

But in the end she admitted it would be wise to try for a big stake so as to give their child the best possible start in life . . .

He hugged and kissed her. 'I'll be thinking of you every day, hon. And Mrs Godfrey next door has promised to look in on you and make sure you're all right.'

'You've got it all arranged, haven't you?' There was a hard edge to her words and he wisely took his leave.

* * *

If Colorado Springs was a little corner of heaven, Cripple Creek was a large portion of hell.

Claims were in short supply, so much so that the authorities rationed them out at only one per man. Of course, teams registered separate claims and thereby gave themselves extra places to work, but no one made any real fuss about that.

Just about anywhere seemed to produce enough gold for a man to live on and, in some cases, to slip away in the middle of the night, hugging a shapeless package, large or small, that contained rich samples hoarded on the quiet.

Not all of them made it away safely . . .

There were gunshots in the night,

sometimes the sounds of a desperate struggle as men fought hand-to-hand until a slim blade slipped between someone's ribs. Others weren't quite so fussy about how they got their gold — a man could fall down a deep shaft with just a nudge. Rocks could tumble with deadly accuracy on a man working his rich vein alone. The sheriff had done his best but was found one morning face down in the creek that ran behind the jail — all cell doors open and not a sign of a prisoner.

Johnny Richards slept at his claim, loaded rifle beside him under his blanket, six-gun in hand across his chest.

The jumpers visited him: just once. He shot the first man through the blanket, hurled it aside, and dropped his two companions with a bullet each. The fourth man fled into the night — a few mornings later he was found dangling at the end of a rope from one of the trees along the creekbank. No one ever found out who had strung him up.

But the businessmen of Cripple Creek didn't like the lawlessness and sent for a US marshal.

He came down from Denver three days later, tacked up notices all over town:

There will be law at Cripple Creek
Break the law, expect to pay
NO EXCEPTIONS

It was signed, *Hart Rebo, US marshal.* By all reports he was as arrogant as ever and Johnny Richards was interested to hear he was still wearing a plaster over his nose. It puzzled him because it was almost two weeks since he had broken that nose — but maybe Hart Rebo had enough of an ego to want the nose properly set by doctors, even slightly reshaped. As he had just come down from Denver to Cripple Creek, this was a distinct possibility, for the big hospital in the Colorado capital had a reputation for doing such operations successfully. They prided themselves on the high standing and skill of their medical staff.

Not that it bothered Richards: he was more worried about how Rebo would react when he discovered him. It was inevitable, even though he was using his mother's maiden name — Chambers — if Rebo made a tour of the diggings . . .

So when he came up out of his shaft just before one sundown as usual to find the marshal sitting on a log in his campsite, smoking a cheroot, he wasn't unduly surprised. The man had one foot hooked over his bent left leg, boot successfully concealing his holster and six-gun from Richards' line of sight. He was smoking with his left hand, removed the cheroot from his mouth now and blew smoke at Richards as he clambered out, begrimed from his day's work, nuggets won held in a knotted kerchief.

Rebo gestured to the bundle. 'Thought it was you — hear you're doin' pretty good.'

'You can leave any time you want, Rebo.' Johnny placed the kerchief of specimens under the end of his bedroll and faced the lawman.

The young lawman's eyes slitted. His right shoulder moved an inch but he wasn't quite ready to try to draw against Richards.

'So you run off, huh? But you can't get away from the marshals. Hell, I just looked at your file, seen your mother's maiden name, checked the claims register and here I am. I tell you, you've made an enemy of Dean Bowen, though. We both got our nuts roasted by the chief marshal 'cause you run out on us. But I had sick time comin' and took it.' He touched his nose plaster lightly. 'Bowen's searchin' high and low for you. If he finds you, he's likely to kill you.'

'That'd suit you, huh?'

'Hell, don't matter to me who kills you.'

Carefully, Richards asked, 'How you holding out for cash? It must be costing plenty to have work done on your nose.'

'Who said I'm gettin' work done on my nose?'

'You mean you want to wear that face I changed for you?'

Rebo didn't like that and his mouth worked, his ears reddened and then he spat. 'You never mind my face, or my money! I can come up with whatever's needed!'

'I was wondering how, that's all.'

'None of your damn business.' Rebo couldn't hide the beginnings of a sly smile. 'I could charge you with assault, you know, get you some jail time.'

'Mebbe . . . but if you decide to, let me know so I can give you damn good cause.'

The marshal let his boot drop back to the ground now and there was even a slight touch of worry in his voice as he said, 'Damn you, Richards! Mebbe I should give out your real name — '

Johnny shook his head. 'You don't want to die that bad.'

'Listen, *mister*, this is official! Din'

you read my dodgers? I'm in charge of these here diggin's now.'

'You swagger around here and you're likely to upset a few men who're a helluva lot tougher than you or the whole damn marshal's outfit combined. Might be lookin' at 'em from the bottom of a mineshaft, Rebo. *They* won't worry about the law, or where they plant their bullets.'

There was an uneasiness in Rebo's eyes that he couldn't hide and Richards knew the man had thought about this, but no doubt hoped his badge, arrogance and confidence might carry him through. But it would take a whole lot more than swagger and a loud voice to deter the claim-jumpers and scum who prowled these diggings after dark.

'I'll be back to check on you, Richards.'

'I'll be here.'

Hart Rebo curled a lip and started to walk away. He paused, looked back over one shoulder, frowning. 'Your claim must be payin' damn good to keep you away from that woman of yours.'

Richards said nothing and Rebo turned and continued to walk away into the dusk, whistling softly now.

That whistle somehow bothered Richards and he wasn't sure why — something about the way Rebo mentioned Joanna and his working this claim in the same breath . . .

He decided he was being too sensitive.

But after supper, he hid the gold he had prised loose from the vein that twisted through his claim like a dancing snake. Then he cleaned and oiled his six-gun: he wore it when working underground, or kept it within reach — either way, the weapon collected dust and moisture.

He picked up his rifle and walked towards the campfires of the other miners scattered widely over the slope and along the creek. He asked in a dozen places but no one had seen the young marshal.

Somehow he was not surprised.

But he didn't want to leave his claim too long unattended, so spoke with Curly Maine and Mitch Damien, two tough young prospectors working just upslope from him. He made a deal with them to guard his claim for a few days.

He wasn't too happy about leaving but he *had* to take the chance while he looked for Hart Rebo.

But Rebo was nowhere to be found in town, and eventually one saloon keeper told him the marshal had ridden out just after sundown.

'Said he had some business in The Springs.'

Those two words had shaken Johnny Richards, made him tighten his grip on his rifle.

The Springs.

Where Jo waited . . . alone.

12

Run for Your Life

It was only a hunch, but one he couldn't afford to ignore.

It had been the slyness on Rebo's face, only partly disguised by the white plaster strips covering his nose. His face was actually swollen a little, from the operations, but that unsettling look was still clear to Richards: the pale blue eyes would have given Hart Rebo away, in any case.

He was planning on going to Colorado Springs to see Joanna! And that 'see' could mean — anything.

All he had to go on was his gut feeling and his observation of the vindictive young marshal's face. But he knew Rebo was going to attack Jo. Maybe Rebo would figure Richards would work it out and come after him

— and maybe that was what he wanted anyway . . .

'Come and watch, you son of a bitch!'

It would be so like that marshal. He had such a twisted mind he would want Johnny Richards to *know* his wife was going to suffer at his hands — know it, and not be able to do anything about it.

Which meant only one thing: Rebo would lie in wait and ambush Richards. But not to kill him — no, that wouldn't set well with the loco thinking of Hart Rebo. He would want Richards to know — be left helpless to wonder and worry, realizing at last that there wasn't a thing he could do to stop it. *He would never reach Joanna in time!*

So Johnny Richards left Cripple Creek as quietly and discreetly as he could, holding to the dark streets and alleys, clearing the hodge-podge town on the northeast side, when the shortest trail to The Springs was to the north*west!*

It meant he had to ride in a wide arc

then to get back to the shorter and most-used trail to Colorado Springs, but he knew this country tolerably well now, having spent quite some time looking it over before he chose his claim.

There was a half-moon and a good deal of rolling clouds which promised rain, so the light varied. He cut the Springs' trail too far to the south. Worried now — *now! Hell he'd been worried since the moment it had come into his head that Rebo was going after Joanna!*

So he raked the sorrel with his spurs, getting a protesting snort and angry snap of the teeth as it swung its head at his leg. But it was a good horse and had always been treated well, knew that if there was now a moment of roughness, there had to be a reason.

So, protest registered, it lengthened its stride and sped on through the night. Richards had good night vision and he picked country that cut bends in the trail when the ground showed few hazards. The clouds rolled on by and the moon came into full view, illuminating the country ahead.

He swung on to the actual trail on a rising slope, knowing there was the wide and deep Cripple Creek beyond: it was a long, meandering watercourse, and there were only one or two places where it was easy to cross.

He swung into the creek before he reached the first of these, giving his horse another reason to snort and whinny as it plunged into a deepwater bend and had to swim for the far bank. Better that than ride into a headshot from Rebo waiting at one of the fords.

But Hart Rebo had used what brains he had and Richards later chastised himself for not acknowledging the fact earlier. The lawman had shown good sense in checking his file and comparing his mother's maiden name with the miners listed on the claims register.

And Rebo had figured Johnny would avoid the regular crossings if he came at all, so waited higher upslope where he could watch both the fords and the deepwater bends.

The sorrel made a large wake, striking out, not liking the deep water in the dark. White foam marked its progress and as the animal heaved, dripping and panting, out on to the bank, Rebo opened fire.

Two quick shots, a pause and then three more. Some bullets zipped into the water, at least one fanned Richards' face, causing him to jerk his head and, instinctively, yank the reins he was holding. He heard the *thunk!* just in front of his face, felt the jerk as the sorrel's head twisted with the impact of the bullet, and then another, softer sound as a third shot took the mount in the neck.

He knew the horse was finished, so kicked his boots free of the stirrups and launched himself to the side, taking the rifle with him.

He landed with a splash at the edge, upper body jarring against the bank. The earth gave way and he slid back into the water — which probably saved his life as two more slugs kicked dirt in front of him. He rolled away from the falling horse, got a foothold and snapped his legs straight, hurling his body up on to the bank. He expected bullets but there were none — he figured Rebo was reloading. Spinning on to his back, he had no trouble locating the ambusher's position: the moonlight touched the gunsmoke with a glow that was as good as a burning match.

Richards triggered a short, savage volley, even seeing the spray of stones and hearing the burring ricochets.

There was no return fire.

Puzzled, Johnny got off two more shots, aiming a little lower. Stones erupted. Lead screamed away into the night. No answering shot!

He knew damn well he hadn't hit Rebo — the man had been reloading and down out of sight and should have filled the magazine by now. Yet still he hadn't returned fire.

Then came a smug, disdainful burst of laughter.

'What'sa matter, Richards? Afoot now . . . ? Sure, you are: I seen to that!' As the laughter died he distinctly heard the creak of saddle leather as Rebo mounted, still well out of sight. 'Me, I'll just mosey on up to The Springs, I reckon — be there by daylight. Aw, you know somethin'? You just missed the train!' A burst of laughter again. 'Heard it whistle roundin' Ballard's Bluff. What a shame! You might've got there ahead of me. Now, well, if you do make it, you can look up that pretty wife of yours first-off, eh?'

Richard's fingers felt as if they were crushing his rifle where he held it. He heard the clatter of hoofs as Rebo spurred away, the man's last words drifting back:

'Well, she *was* mighty *pretty* when you saw her last! See what you think when you next see her, you son of *a bitch!*'

Johnny threw the rifle to his shoulder

but held his fire at the last second: it would be a futile gesture. The man was having his revenge for that crushed nose now. Setting Richards afoot, *telling* him he was going to attack his wife, *knowing* there was nothing Richards could do to prevent him.

Or was there?

The train! The good old Denver and Rio Grande, linking Denver and Colorado Springs, thanks to the general's foresight and money and the 'goodwill' he had spread among the right people who agreed to run a spur track up to The Springs.

If, as Rebo said, the train had whistled going round Ballard's Bluff it would be going away from where he now stood — *but it had to swing back*, lower down the bluff, and that was to his advantage: swing back on to the line that cut almost as straight as a pencil across country leading to The Springs. If he could reach it before it started that last long, zigzag climb up Pikes Peak . . .

He reloaded the rifle, snatched a spare box of cartridges from the sodden saddle-bags, paused an instant to pat the head of the dead, once-faithful mount, and then started off at a jogtrot.

Rebo was long gone although a little dust still hung in the air from his passage. Richards didn't bother looking for any sign of the man. He concentrated on the Bluff, rearing in black silhouette against the moontouched clouds. As he drew closer, lungs burning now with effort, he smelled the smoke from the train. He couldn't hear it because of the blood pounding in his ears: it would be round the far side of the bluff now, anyway. He tried to recall a picture of the bluff, where the rail line dropped down in its gentle curve to the flat ground. A dry riverbed ran beside it for a spell, some brush, a lift in the ground, with several boulders — *Damn!* He couldn't recall what was beyond that.

But he would make the boulders his target: if he could get to the top of one he could drop on to the train as it passed below him . . .

He hadn't paused in his run, never broke stride, even though his legs, especially his ankles, were ready to snap. He felt the drag of the rifle now: it was pulling him off-balance, over to his left, and he had to regularly compensate for this so he didn't veer too far from the direction he had set himself. *All right!* He let the rifle fall, hearing the clatter and slide as it spilled down a gravelly slope.

Now he was moving better, faster! He was running more erect, arms working like pistons, helping pump air into his aching lungs. Sweat stung his eyes and he flung it off with an irritable sweep of one hand or the other. His leg muscles were screaming for rest . . .

What was that? A flash of some kind . . .

Just for an instant he wondered if Rebo had outguessed him, ridden here, laid low and in wait, going to shoot him just as he figured he would reach the train and — No! The flash was moonlight running along the polished top of twin metal tracks — *the railroad . . .*

It was slightly above him and the tracks dipped, swung in a sharp curve. He made himself pause, bending double, clenching the stitch in his side, gulping down great, gulps of air, all of which deadened his hearing. He couldn't tell if the train was *coming or going* away from him. *Stupid!* You'd see it if it had already reached this point!

He hadn't even realized he was moving again, staggering now, feeling the ground rising slowly but inevitably under his pounding boots. His feet ached and burned; no doubt skin had been rubbed raw, but no time to think about that. There were the first of the boulders! *Too damn low and not close enough to the track.*

Weaving like a Saturday night drunk, he was startled to find he was moving with a crab-like motion, bent over, fingers clawing into the steep ground for purchase, boots scrabbling behind,

thrusting him up the slope — up
— up . . .

He fell on his face.

His breath raised puffs of dust that
stung his eyes, clogged his nostrils.
His heart thudded against the ground.
He was trembling — needed more
— air . . .

No! He wasn't trembling: the ground
was.

And in the same instant he heard the
screaming whistle of the locomotive as
it swayed under a stream of belching
black smoke and sparks around the
bend and started up what was, to it, a
neglible rise.

*How did he get to the top of the
damn boulder?* He had no recollection
of it at all and now wasn't the time to
worry about it. He coughed and choked
as he was engulfed in a massive thick
shroud of black smoke and his eyes
streamed. He saw the blurred amber glow
of the locomotive's firebox, the stacked
lengths of firewood in the tender, heard
the clank of the couplings, saw the dim

blur of windows, a ridged roof that, was suddenly rising towards him.

Then there was a thud that drove what little breath he had left from his body and his fingers clawed wildly at the ridges, legs swinging over the edge of the swaying car.

With an effort he didn't realize he could make, he dragged himself to the middle of the roof and, splayed out like a crucifix, hugged the plank walkway as the locomotive whistled again and the train hurtled down on to the shining track below as it ran like twin arrows towards the distant Springs.

He tightened the drawstring of his hat under his chin and ducked his head for a little less air-resistance.

★   ★   ★

He had some luck: not only because he didn't topple off the roof of the swaying van as the train took the curves before gathering speed for the straight run, but because it was a mixed passenger freight. This meant the train stopped in the freight yards first and unhooked the flatbed wagons, then rode the passengers in to the depot for disembarking.

The depot was only a few blocks from the house he had rented for Joanna and it was just getting light. He judged, quite accurately that it was about 5 a.m., the time he had been starting his mining, getting as much done in the cool of early morning as he could before the heat of day made it difficult to work.

So he clambered down over the tender and the driver and engineer stiffened, the engineer raising a large spanner, blocking his way as he went to climb down to the footplate.

'That ride'll cost you, feller. We don't run this railroad for freeloaders.'

' 'Course you don't,' agreed Richards and dug two small pellets of gold from his pocket. 'Here — buy yourself a beer.'

They were suspicious but the driver whistled. 'A beer? Hell, I'll be able to buy the weekend supplies with this. Say, feller, you need a hand diggin' wherever you got this?'

Now at the foot of the steps, Johnny looked up and grinned. 'Won it in a card game — thanks for the ride.'

'You goin' far? There's a small corral behind the water tank with a few hosses that drunken cowboys left and forgot about. You want, I can walk down with you and tell 'em to give you one.'

That suited Johnny Richards and within minutes he was riding the back streets towards the rented house. He passed Mrs Godfrey's, saw the grey-haired woman moving about her kitchen by lamplight. He swung wide around a small garden toolshed and came to the back yard of his rented house.

He tensed when he saw a horse tethered to one of the lemon trees, its coat dark with patches of sweat. The same bay Hart Rebo had been riding, if he wasn't mistaken . . .

He slid off the bare back of the borrowed mount, loosened his six-gun in leather as he hurried across the yard to the back door. He glanced down the side of the house towards the street at the front and sucked in a sharp breath: there were two more horses hitched to the front picket fence.

At the same moment this registered, he heard a muffled cry from inside, the sound of breaking glass, like a jar or ornament falling, and *men's* voices, too low for him to make out what they were saying.

He ran to the back door, was about to kick it in but recalled there was a short passage that led down to the parlour and anyone there — where he was sure the cry and voices had come from — would be waiting to pick him off.

The door was unlocked and he automatically cursed: he'd told Jo before he left *always* to keep the damn doors and windows locked when she was alone! He realized it hardly mattered now. Just then there was the dull, hammerblow of a gunshot from the parlour and this time Jo let out a scream that chilled his blood.

Not worrying about noise now he lunged down the passage to the arched doorway of the parlour, saw a man curled up on the floor clutching his midriff. Jo was being held by Rebo and there was a smoking Colt in his hand. A third man crouched in the shadows by a credenza and he swung his gun towards Richards as the man dived in headlong.

He twisted in mid air as Rebo's gun and that of the crouched man blazed. Lead tugged at the left sleeve of his shirt. He swung the gun past Rebo and Jo and triggered at the man in the shadows as he reared up and took a step forward, shooting.

Richards dropped to one knee, fired and the man was hurled back by the lead, crashed into the credenza and fell face down on the floor.

Joanna screamed his name.

He swung that way as he lifted to his knees but froze even as he started to cock the hammer.

Rebo had his gun barrel pushed up under Joanna's ribs and she lifted to her toes in an effort to take some of the pressure off.

'Drop it, Richards! *Drop it!*'

Johnny let his gun fall and lifted his open hands out from his sides. 'All right, Rebo. You've got me cold. Let her go now.'

Hart Rebo half-smothered a laugh at the suggestion.

'You are one cock-eyed optimist, mister! This is just what I wanted. Now you can watch while I have me some fun with *your wife!* But you won't be able to do a thing about it, because first I'm gonna cripple you — like — this . . .'

He lifted his gun away from the woman and slanted the barrel down so that it pointed at Johnny's midriff, dropped a little lower, and inched towards his left hip.

'Man, they say gettin' a bullet smack-damn in the hipbone is *ex-cruciatin*'! Said to make grown men cry. Let's see if it's true, huh . . .?'

'No!'

Joanna screamed the word right against Rebo's ear and the man literally jumped a foot into the air, spinning away, head ringing with the shock of the explosive sound so close.

He reeled, his balance briefly affected, and by then Richards was rolling, scooping up his Colt and triggering from floor level. The tattoo of three rapid shots and Rebo was twisting and jerking like someone was pulling wires attached to his lean body. He fell, his pale blue eyes widened above the plaster strips covering his nose as he ploughed face-first on to the floor . . .

His boots were still drumming fitfully when Johnny vaulted to his feet and ran to the white-faced, sagging Joanna.

She clung to him, her knees weak, and he half carried her to the small sofa and laid her on it, blood from the bullet welt on his left arm smearing her torn frock.

'Easy, hon — it's OK now . . . '

'No!' she cried, and he was about to

argue when she pointed past him and opened her mouth to scream again. He tumbled away from her, swinging his still-hot Colt, saw the man by the credenza on his knees, a gun held in both shaking hands, aimed at Joanna.

There were two bullets left in Johnny's gun and he put both of them into Greg Hammond's heaving chest.

He hastily reloaded, thumbing in cartridges, watching Hammond stretch out and lie still, his hate-filled eyes dulling swiftly. Richards snapped the loading gate closed and put the gun on the third man.

He had been shot in the chest, dead now, a complete stranger to Richards. He went to Jo who clung to him and he sat down on the sofa with her, held her as she trembled violently. When she had settled a little he gave her a little brandy from a decanter on the sideboy, and asked, 'All right now?'

She shook her head slightly, clutching the empty glass. 'Not really — but I — I will be.'

'Who is that feller lying by Hammond?'

'One of his gunmen, I think. He called him Derby.' She shuddered. 'Oh, God, Johnny it was — horrible.'

He saw the bruises for the first time then on the side of her face, and upper chest. One sleeve had been torn away and there were deep, colouring finger-marks showing against her pale flesh. He felt anger rising.

'How the *hell* did he find you?'

'Through Rebo — Greg Hammond was in the same hospital as him in Denver. Hammond had a heart problem. Rebo boasted how he had bled him for a thousand dollars, cash on the spot, told him you were at Cripple Creek, then said for another thousand, he could arrange for you to come here, and could catch you and — watch while they — I — ' She paused, and he felt her heart banging against her ribs, tightened his arm about her shoulders. 'Hammond knew he was a dying man and wanted to kill you himself, but — but he wanted you to live — long — enough to see what — they did to me. Rebo shot the gunman who got mad when Rebo tried to get that extra thousand out of Hammond, then wounded Greg who tried to — to — '

He caught her as she started to topple and eased her back on to the sofa, gently lifting her feet up. 'It's OK, Jo — I can figure the rest and — '

He spun, Colt blurring into his right hand, as the door opened and a hard-breathing man stepped inside.

Marshal Dean Bowen stood there, hand on gun butt.

He raked his wild-looking eyes around the room. 'Goddamn! Just too late! By God! I dunno why I ever worried about Hammond's men gettin' to you, Richards! *He* was the one needed protection!'

'You're short a man now,' Richards told him gesturing to Rebo.

Bowen's face remained blank. 'No loss. Vindictive and too damn cocky to ever have made a good marshal. Even left me a note crowing about how he figured out how to find you, and if I wanted to come to The Springs he'd show me just how good he was. I'd've found you all right: as a corpse.'

'Disappointed?'

Bowen glared then smiled crookedly, shook his head. 'Guess not.' He gestured to the sprawled corpse of Greg Hammond. 'He quit the Denver Hospital against doctor's orders, with that gunnie, Walt Derby. The docs were worried about his health and got in touch with me. I figured he had to be where Hart had traced you to — and here you are.' He heaved a sigh, still very deadpan. 'Well, one thing, you won't gimme any more headaches tryin' to find somewhere safe for you and your wife. Nothin' more for you to worry about now. You can start living an ordinary life — no more problems.'

Richards slid his arm about Jo's waist and smiled down at her. 'I wouldn't say that,' he said and she snapped her head up, face anxious. His smile broadened. 'I dunno a thing about babies.'

She turned her face into his chest,

240

and there was a brief, muffled sound of laughter.

'Well, don't look at me!' Bowen said. Then his lips moved in a silent curse. 'Hell, you may not have any real problems, but you've still given me some.' He glared at Johnny Richards. 'I'm going to be up to my elbows in paperwork tryin' to explain away this mess.' He turned abruptly. 'Might's well go get started, I reckon — I'll send someone for the bodies.'

He opened the door, shaking his head dolefully.

'I think he really enjoys having something to complain about,' Jo said in a low voice.

Johnny looked down into her upturned face. He winked and she smiled as she clung to him.

Bowen opened the door, still muttering.

Richards called just before the door closed: 'We kinda owe you somethin', for running out on you — after you tried to find us a safe place to hide, Bowen.'

'Hardly matters now, does it?' the marshal asked bluntly, starting to close the door.

'If it's a boy, we thought we'd call him 'Dean'.'

The door opened again a few inches and Bowen's stern face peered in at them. He saw Richards look quizzically at his pale and bruised wife, and she smiled slowly as she nodded.

'It sounds nice — Dean Richards,' she said quietly.

'You'd really call him — after me?' Bowen said frowning.

'Well, only if you agree . . . '

Then, for the first time since they'd known him, they watched Dean Bowen's long face break into a wide smile, almost ear-to-ear.

THE END